A HOLE IN THE HEAD

Some other books by the same author

A Rag, a Bone and a Hank of Hair
Backlash
Dark Sun, Bright Sun
Grinny
Living Fire
Monster Maker
On the Flip Side
Robot Revolt
Snatched
Sweets from a Stranger
The Talking Car
Time Trap
Trillions
You Remember Me!
The Worm Charmers

A HOLE
IN
THE HEAD

NICHOLAS FISK

WALKER BOOKS
LONDON

First published 1991 by Walker Books Ltd
87 Vauxhall Walk, London SE11 5HJ

© 1991 Nicholas Fisk

First printed 1991

Printed in Great Britain by
Billings and Son Ltd, Worcester

British Library Cataloguing in Publication Data
Fisk, Nicholas
A hole in the head.
I.Title
823'.914 [F]   PZ7

ISBN 0-7445-1942-X

CONTENTS

A DOG, BARKING

In that grey-white wilderness, featureless and blank, there was nothing to see. Not even a horizon.

And, other than the hiss of wind-driven powder snow, nothing to hear. Nothing except –

The barking of a dog! Impossible! But listen... Somewhere, a dog was barking, barking, barking.

"Where is it?" Madi said, jerking her head from side to side. "I can only hear it, I can't *see* anything!"

Jonjo wiped powder snow from his sister's vizor and said, "Over there! It's got to be there! The MetrePak!"

Now she could just make it out: a MetrePak. A standard-issue metal cube exactly one metre square, standing all alone. The dull yellow of its walls was almost bleached white by clinging snow. The MetrePak seemed to come and go, vanish and reappear in the icy swirl.

And the dog kept barking, barking, barking.

"We've got to do something!" Madi said. "Poor thing, it's tearing its throat to pieces!"

Jonjo stood still and said nothing. He was

twelve, old enough to be cautious. Madi was two years younger, young enough to be reckless. She tugged at his arm.

"Please, Jonjo!" she said. "*Please!*"

Jonjo thought, Might as well do what she says. Can't just stand here. Stay still, and your face aches and your fingers stiffen. The cold cuts right into you...

"Come on!" she said, and trotted towards the MetrePak. She couldn't run properly, of course: not in all those layers of auto-heated clothes. He shambled after her. With each step, snow hissed and whispered beneath their boots.

They reached the MetrePak. A curved wedge of snow sealed the lid, but it was not locked. Jonjo pushed his thickly-gloved fingers into the recessed handle and pulled. The lid came away. The MetrePak was open.

And there was the dog. Chained to a metal upright. It stopped barking – pulled at its chain, trying to reach them – and stood on its hind legs, scrabbling desperately.

"Good dog," Madi said, moving forward. "Nice dog."

Jonjo held her back. "Careful!" he said.

The dog frantically lunged at them. It twisted its head and gaped its mouth as if it were having a fit. Its collar strangled its throat. Its eyes rolled.

"Good boy," Jonjo said. He kept his voice

low and steady. "What's your name, eh? Have you got a name?" Very slowly, he stretched out a hand protected by four thicknesses of fabric.

The dog seemed to have something stuck in its throat. It gasped, mouthed, swung its head. It gaped and showed sharp white teeth. Then, as if it were being sick, it brought up words.

The dog spoke.

"Good dog!" it said. "Good dog good!"

"A talking dog!" Jonjo said. "It's impossible! We're dreaming!"

"He's having the same dream," Madi said. "Just listen to him!"

Its name was Bob. It told Jonjo and Madi so.

It was a good dog: it kept saying so, rolling humble eyes. They fed it all the food their suits carried. The dog wolfed everything, even bits of wrapping.

"Back to OzBase, right?" Jonjo said to Madi. She nodded. After all, there was nowhere else to go. But she, like Jonjo, was uneasy. Who had locked the dog in the MetrePak? Who had deliberately left it out there to die?

They followed their own footsteps in the snow. The dog walked with them – or rather pranced, danced, ran in circles. It was mad with joy. It licked their gloved hands. "Bob

9

good dog!" it said, twisting and choking with the effort.

When they were nearly home, Madi stopped. She was frowning. She knelt by the dog, tousled its head, looked up at Jonjo and said, "We've got to know more, we can't just walk in with *him*..." Jonjo nodded. "Ask him what it's all about," he said.

Madi took the dog's paw, shook it gently and said, "Why were you left out there, Bob?"

The dog took time to think out this question. It looked from face to face, panting white puffs of breath, its body tense.

At last it said, "Left lone box."

"Yes, that's right, you were left alone out there. Why, Bob? Why?"

"Bob lone," said the dog. Then, effortfully, "Man bad."

"So a bad man put you there? Did you do something wrong, Bob? Did you bite someone? Were you bad?"

"Bob good dog! *Good dog!*" – almost barking.

"Then why, Bob?"

"Cos," the dog replied, twisting its neck with the effort to make words, "cos ... Bob talk. Talk-dog bad."

It looked sadly from Jonjo's eyes to Madi's, from Madi's to Jonjo's; then it asked, "Is Bob ... bad?"

Madi answered by flinging her arms round

Bob's neck. The dog trembled with pleasure, wagged its tail and tried to lick her face. It made whimpering, puppy noises. Jonjo looked on. "Don't you start howling, Madi!" he warned his sister. "You know what happens to tears!"

"I'm not crying," she lied; and quickly rubbed at her eyes. Tears froze. Removing them could be painful.

"Better get on," Jonjo said, nodding his head at the one distant light in the endless, colourless blankness surrounding them.

The light came from OzBase – Ozone-layer Research Base – where an international team of scientists investigated the hole in the Arctic's Ozone Layer. OzBase was a low scatter of big and small hutments, a little colony so isolated that it needed to show a beacon in that frozen immensity. When the Arctic winds blew, and snow swirled like ghosts, you could blink your frozen eyelids and OzBase was gone...

"Let's move," Jonjo said. "I'm beginning to seize up." He flailed his arms. They moved closer to OzBase. At first, Bob enjoyed himself, pulling at his chain, dragging Madi along. But once or twice he lifted his head, sniffed in the direction of the Base, and grumbled uneasily. "He's saying 'Man bad'," Madi murmured to Jonjo. "He's remembering where his troubles started. He's afraid of a bad man in OzBase."

"Why OzBase?" said Jonjo.

"Well, it must be. I mean, Bob's *here*, so I suppose —"

Jonjo shrugged. "In any case, the Base is our only place to go," he said. "And Mum's there, she'll sort it out."

"No, she's not," Madi said. "She left yesterday."

"So she did," Jonjo said. "She's in OzTech Centre. Back in civilization. Norway…" He rubbed his nose to prevent icicles forming. "And the chopper that took her away brought in five new people, right? I'll bet one of them was responsible for…" He nodded at the dog.

Bob was too intelligent to miss Jonjo's meaning. "Man bad," he said. "Man put Bob BOX." His tail drooped.

Jonjo and Madi gazed at the dog. He was a handsome animal. Mostly border collie, but with a thicker coat patched with brown and black on white fur. Without that thicker coat he would not have survived his captivity. His chestnut-coloured eyes were bright with intelligent emotions – affection, anxiety, willingness to please, questioning.

"I just can't imagine how *anyone* could want to … you know…" Madi said; and yet again caressed the dog's head.

"Me neither," said Jonjo. He tried to puzzle it out. Five new arrivals: had one come alone, separately? Yes, definitely. Because whoever had ditched Bob would have had to arrive complete with the MetrePak and Bob. The Pak must have been let down from the chopper, with Bob inside.

But wouldn't Bob have barked? Wouldn't the pilot have asked questions?

And why not simply shoot Bob, or poison him? Why go to all the trouble of transporting him here, and marooning him in a MetrePak?

No answer.

Next question: how would he and Madi identify the person responsible? Could be difficult. You haven't even seen the new arrivals, he told himself; and if you had seen them, it wouldn't help. New arrivals are just bundles of clothing when they first arrive. And in any case, you seldom get to know anyone really well. People come and go all the time – doctors, dentists, technicians, scientists and all kinds of "-ologists"...

But mostly scientists, of course. Because of the Hole in the Head, the hole in the Ozone Layer over the Arctic.

First there had been a hole in earth's atmosphere over the South Pole, the Antarctic. Now the same thing had happened in the Arctic – in the north. The scientists had to find out what was happening; why there was a hole; if it was getting bigger; what it could mean; what to do about it.

But Jonjo had to find out who had tried to kill Bob. Finding out would not be easy.

Madi was saying, "Oh, if only Mum were here!"

Jonjo did not bother to reply. Mum wasn't here, she was *there*, back in civilization. Big conference – "I've *got* to go, back soon, enjoy yourselves, be good!" Right now, she'd be wearing a *dress* and *stockings*, would you believe, and choosing food from a *menu* in a *dining-room*.

Mum was a world away.

And Dad? Dad had walked out on them two years ago and become the invisible man.

They reached OzBase, stuffed their codecards into the slot, saw the first and second doors open, felt the almost shocking warmth of the Centre's air – and were home. The Check-in and Locker Room areas were empty, as usual. They stripped themselves of all their gear and unclipped Bob's chain.

The dog began to whimper and turn its head this way and that. "Don't be afraid, Bob!" Jonjo said. "We'll take care of you."

Bob rolled his eyes.

"Just keep very quiet," Madi told Bob. "Not a sound. Understand?"

Bob sorted out her words and finally nodded his head. "I've taught him to nod instead of trying to speak," Madi said proudly.

14

"A nod for yes; a shake for no. That's it, isn't it, Bob?"

Bob nodded his head. Then, with his tail curled between his hind legs and the whites of his eyes showing, he crawled under a bench and hid himself.

TOP SUSPECT

Four of the five new arrivals were in the lounge – the only sizeable, crowded, welcoming place in OzBase. There were three new men, all "-ologists" of some sort; and a new woman who turned out to be a computer and statistics whizz. Madi and Jonjo learned these facts by listening to the excited conversations at the bar.

Madi's eyes flicked from face to face. Her lips were tightly pursed, her eyes glittered. She was sizing up the new arrivals, looking for the "bad man".

It took her only a minute or so to select her victim.

"That's him!" she hissed.

"Who's him?" Jonjo said.

"Him. The one who locked up poor Bob."

Jonjo said, "Hold on! Let me find out if he arrived alone in a chopper. Because if he did —"

Madi waved him aside. "Never mind all that," she said. "That's *him*. I *know*. The nasty little drip!"

Jonjo studied the man. "Drip" was right. He was small, tense, untidily balding, bony-fingered and furtive. When someone made a

16

joke – and everyone was talking loudly, excited by the new arrivals – the man gave a rabbity grin that came seconds too late.

Madi made straight for him, sat herself down beside him and said, quietly but distinctly, "*Dogs*. Do you like dogs?"

"Dogs?" the little man replied. "You mean, *dogs*? Yes, I suppose I like dogs."

"No, you don't," Madi said.

"I'm sorry, I'm not with you…"

"You don't like dogs," Madi said calmly. "You're a dog-killer."

The little man's eyes flicked from side to side, looking for an escape; but Madi had him pinned.

"One particular dog," she said. "You killed him, right?"

"A lie! I never killed that dog!" the man said.

Madi pounced. "What dog didn't you kill?" she said. "The dog in the MetrePak? Name of Bob?"

"Go away," the man said miserably. He seemed to have shrunk even smaller. And now Jonjo sat on the other side of the man, hemming him in. "What sort of person," Jonjo said, "would try to kill a beautiful animal in that – that —"

"Disgusting, cowardly way?" Madi said.

"*Try* to kill it?" the man said. "You mean the dog's still *alive*?"

"No thanks to you," Madi said.

The man said, "Oh, my God! Where can we go to talk?"

But at that moment, the last of the new arrivals made her entrance...

Dr Inge Lindstrom.

The babble of conversation in the lounge dwindled – stumbled – stopped. All eyes fastened upon Dr Lindstrom. The expressions in the eyes of the men were very different from those in the women's; for Inge Lindstrom was even more gorgeous in the flesh than on the TV screen.

Typically, she had taken the time to change her outfit. The other new arrivals still wore anoraks, parkas, sweaters: Inge wore a softly clinging, pure white dress, a gold belt round her small waist and a number of gold bangles on a golden wrist.

"And those eyes...!" someone muttered.

Indeed, Inge's eyes were something of a feature. The lashes were very black, the whites very white and the irises an astonishing, piercing, ice-blue. The rest of her – her limbs, mouth, body, teeth – was merely perfect.

"Why, Inge!" cried the big Canadian, his voice too hearty, his smile too wide.

"Why, Bud! Bud Mackenzie!" replied Inge, with just the right degree of enthusiasm. He opened his arms to give her a bear-hug. She smoothly avoided it. "And Linda, Hammond,

Françoise, Paul, Dr Chow, Dr Gonzales!" she beamed, getting every name right instantly. "Oh, but this is to be a busman's holiday, is that how you say it? All my most favourite colleagues!"

Jonjo could not take his eyes off her.

Madi could. She studied the little man beside her. Seeing his face flush, his eyes stare and pop, she thought, Oh yes! Another worshipper!

"Terrific, isn't she?" Madi said in the little man's ear. "And so famous! And always on TV – those peakview science programmes! And so beautiful! Don't you think she's super? Aren't you lucky to have such a gorgeous boss?" She stabbed the questions at him, testing him.

The little man slowly turned his head to Madi. Now his eyes stared straight into hers: eyes glazed with bafflement, worry, even fear.

"We've got to get away from here!" he said. "Got to *talk*! Where can we go?"

They led the man to Madi's tiny bedroom because it was tidier than Jonjo's. The man sat on the only chair and Madi and Jonjo sat on the bed.

"I suppose you're wondering who I am," the man said, sullenly.

"No, I'm not," Madi said. "I checked out all the expected arrivals days ago on the computer. I'm great at prying and probing.

19

You're either the geophysicist or the psychologist, right?"

"The psychologist," the man said.

"Big-deal *psychologist*," Jonjo sneered. "Fat lot of good you'll do up here." The man bit his lower lip.

"Why would you want to kill Bob?" Madi said, pouncing once again.

The man leaned back in his uncomfortable chair and took a deep breath. "Listen," he said at last, "I've got to try to make you understand some difficult things."

"Like why you tried to kill poor Bob," Madi said.

"Things you'll find hard to believe," the man said, ignoring her. "Things about yourselves, the dog and this place." He smoothed his scanty hair, rubbed his chin. "I'll start with this place."

Jonjo said, "We know all about this place. It's an international research centre trying to find out what causes the Hole; and what the Hole causes; and what's to be done about it."

"So you know the damage the Hole seems to be causing so far?" the man said.

"Of course. It lets more sunlight through, which means more ultraviolet radiation. Which could mean more skin cancers among humans, and effects on animal and plant life. And the polar ice-cap could start to melt, and climate and sea-levels alter —"

"Look, just take it that we know all that stuff," Madi said. "I mean, who *doesn't?*"

"Anything else you know?" the man said.

"We could go on for ever if we wanted to," Jonjo said. "But we don't. Greenhouse Effect, aerosols, the Polar Vortex, you want a lecture on them? Chemical interactions within the stratosphere, biological feedbacks —"

"Mummy is a top scientist, ever so clever!" Madi lisped, mock-childishly. "Daddy too. So us kiddywinks are ever so clever too."

"All right, all right," the man said. "Obviously you know all about the direct, observable effects of the Hole. But then there are the lateral connections to consider."

"Lateral Thinking," Madi interrupted. "Believe it or not, we know about that too. Let's see, now... Lateral connections... Some maniac hits me on the head with a hammer, OK? That's a direct injury, a complete action. Jonjo hears about it and gets in a panic —"

"Not a chance," Jonjo said. "I'd cheer."

"Ha-ha. Jonjo gets in a panic, jumps on his bike and pedals furiously to the hospital. But because he's in a state, he doesn't look where he's going and a car hits him. And that's a lateral connection."

"And that's why I am here," the man said. "To observe lateral connections of the Hole. They think psychologists are best for that sort of thing. So do I."

21

For the first time he seemed less of a weed, more of a person. There was a silence.

Madi said, "What about Bob? Is he a lateral connection? Is he a psychological problem? And do you sort it out by killing him? A poor dog, a beautiful dog like that! Murderer! Pig!"

The man said, "Oh, hell!" and stood up. "I came with you to *talk*, not to be cross-examined. My name is Max Gibbon, Dr Max Gibbon, how do you do and goodbye." He opened the door.

"No wait, what about Bob?" Jonjo said.

"You worry about him," Max said. "I've had him up to *here*. He's all yours. Just keep him hidden."

The door closed and he was gone.

Jonjo and Madi stared at each other. Jonjo said, "Perhaps he *wasn't* Bob's murderer?"

Madi said, "I quite liked him when he lost his temper."

Jonjo shook his head wonderingly at her, then said, "We'd better see to Bob."

OzBase was all corridors, like a train, leading from one complex of huts to another. All the corridors were finished in standard dove grey. As Jonjo and Madi entered and left them, warm air wafted across their faces. The air smelled of dust, or electricity, or cooking fat, or chemicals, or bathrooms, according to where they were. The arrowed direction signs

were hardly necessary. You could navigate by
smell, or – if you wanted to reach the only big
building, the lounge – by noise. Jonjo and
Madi paused for a moment outside the
circular window in one of the lounge's doors
and looked in.

The usual gathering had become a party.
Everyone held drinks, everyone was laughing,
talking, sweating. And all heads were turned
in the direction of the star of the party – Inge
Lindstrom. She was drinking, talking,
laughing; but she was not sweating. She was
looking coolly beautiful. "Oh, no!" she was
saying. "Oh no, that cannot be true! So they
are married? She is so big, so very tall, and he
is only – how do you say? – a little titchy man!
A ladder he would need!"

Roars of laughter from all the men.
Unwilling smiles from the only three women at
OzBase – a computer specialist and two
communications administrators.

"Isn't she just great!" Jonjo smirked.

"Great," Madi agreed. "Great *cow*."
Scowling, she pulled Jonjo away. "We're
supposed to be seeing to Bob," she said.

The dog had left the seat under which he had
been hiding. They watched him through the
window: now he was trotting back and forth,
mouth half open, eyes rolling to show anxious
whites.

"Ah, poor Bob!" Madi said, kneeling to stroke the dog's head. "What's the matter, then?"

"This is the matter," Jonjo said, pointing to a corner of the little room. There was a wet patch on the floor. "Puddle of piddle," Jonjo said.

Bob made a strangled, hooting noise and said, "Bob bad dog."

"No, you're not, of course you're not!" Madi said. But Bob would not be consoled. He made anxious noises, half whine and half yelp, and wriggled his rear end.

"He wants to do some more," Jonjo said. He frowned. "Something we hadn't thought of. Hell..."

Madi said, "Check that the corridor is clear. We'll get him to the loo by our bedrooms. Quick."

"What are we going to *do*?" Madi said, as they hurried through corridors. "I mean, we can't just take him for walks three times a day, and we can't *dispose* of anything."

"Potty training," Jonjo said. "He'll have to learn to use our loos."

"But *how*?" Madi said. "He won't *fit*."

With the aid of the lid of a suitcase, bashed into shape – and the helping hands of Jonjo and Madi – Bob learned to use the loo.

It began seriously enough. Bob struggled,

scrabbled, slipped, lost one leg down the
S-bend, rolled his eyes, trembled with anxiety
to please ... and at last was perched in a
crouching attitude over the pan. The suitcase
lid helped. His paws and claws did not slip
on it.

"Good dog, Bob!" Madi said. "There you
are at last! Now *perform*!" But Bob could not.

He looked from Madi to Jonjo and back
again. His rear quarters trembled. He
produced small woofing noises. But nothing
else.

He looked so ridiculous perched on the pot
that Jonjo began to giggle: then Madi. Bob
went on looking agonized.

"I know!" Madi said. "We'll get out. Leave
him alone. Leave him to it."

They waited outside the door as if they were
hospital visitors, trying to look serious and
respectable. But they could not stop smothered
bursts of giggles.

At last they heard a solitary "Woof!" and a
thumping noise. They entered the room.

Now Bob was sitting on the floor, head held
high. The thumping noise was made by his tail
wagging against the unwanted suitcase lid.
"Ah, he's smiling!" Madi said. She rushed to
embrace him while Jonjo pressed the knob
that flushed the pan.

By the end of the next day, Bob had even
learned to press the knob himself. Also to

balance on the pan. To show his pride and pleasure, he ceremoniously pulled the suitcase lid to pieces with his teeth. Then he sat among the pieces and said, "Bob good dog."

They found a hiding place for Bob in a little stationery store-room near their bedrooms. "But it's not good enough," Madi said. "It's not *safe*. I know that hardly anyone ever goes there, but all the same –"

"I know, I know," said Jonjo. He looked unhappy. "Dogs need exercise, dogs need entertainment – and dogs *smell*. You can hide the dog but you can't hide the dog-smell. Not for ever. I don't know..."

"And Dr Max Gibbon has washed his hands of the whole thing," Madi said. "You'd have thought that with his guilty conscience, he'd do something to help."

Jonjo thought about this. Then he said, "Hang on. He *can't* just wash his hands, can he? Not if we don't let him. We can *use* him, *make* him help us. If we told all the others what we know, he'd be mud, wouldn't he?"

"You're right," Madi said. "Let's *hound* him, let's *dog* him, ha-ha."

"Ha-ha and ho-ho," Jonjo said, jumping to his feet. "Come on then."

They found Max easily. He was in the lounge. But also in the lounge they found Dr Inge

26

Lindstrom and at least a dozen male adorers, all acting manly and laughing loudly.

Max saw Madi and Jonjo enter. He had been sitting alone with an untouched drink in his hands. At once he got up and joined the others. He lost himself among them. "Clever, very clever," Jonjo muttered.

"I'll get to him," Madi said fiercely. She pushed her way through to Dr Lindstrom and said, loudly and clearly, "Hello. You are Dr Inge Lindstrom. I am Madi Bligh and this is my brother Jonjo. How do you do."

"Oh! How very nice," cried Dr Lindstrom. "I have heard about you so much! And your parents, of course I know of them, what scientist does not!" She beamed radiant smiles, shook hands, cooed compliments, offered drinks.

Madi scowled. Jonjo grinned clownishly and turned pink.

"I have met your father, oh yes, quite a number of times, Helsinki, London, San Francisco," Inge said, speaking exclusively to Jonjo. She continued to hold and shake his hand. "Do you know something? – You are *very* like him! Oh, *very* like!" She purred the words. Jonjo went pinker.

Madi, left out, scowled even more fiercely.

Still holding his hand, Inge led him to one of the long seats by the wall. They sat.

"Ah!" said Inge, "and here is another old

friend, Dr Max Gibbon! Always so distant, you would not think him my friend! But you are, aren't you, Max?" She patted the seat with her long-fingered, tanned hand.

Max sat down. He began to sweat.

"May I join the party?" Madi said. She crashed a chair down in front and thumped her bottom on to it.

Inge seemed not to see her. She glittered at Max, dazzled Jonjo, ignored Madi. Max mumbled something and got up to go. Inge pulled him down again. Now Max's sweating face seemed swollen. Madi glowered and muttered, "Mousy Max. Caught in the mantrap. Stupid git." Only Jonjo heard.

"Such a day!" Inge enthused. "A new friend," (she patted Jonjo's hand) "and an old friend!" (she patted Max's). Max winced, stood up and this time escaped.

Madi went out with him. "Well, well, well!" she said. "True love at last! Lucky you! Lovely love! Yum yum!"

Max jerked to a halt so suddenly that Madi almost tripped over his feet. He thrust his face at Madi and began swearing. He used words people don't use in front of children. When he had finished he muttered, "Sorry. Inexcusable. But that woman...! She's straight poison. I could kill her."

PSYCHO-CERAMIC

Though they did not dare take Bob outside, Madi and Jonjo did their best to exercise him. But their best wasn't good enough. Not that Bob complained. Loyal and obliging, he "went for a good run" – he hurtled up and down the long corridor of the sleeping quarters, almost certain to be empty during the day. Jonjo would run with Bob while Madi kept watch or vice versa.

Bob pretended he was having the time of his life. He scrabbled, skidded, flailed his tail, made mock attacks at ankles. He did everything a dog being exercised should do, except bark. He was too clever to bark, he understood the danger of discovery.

He was not clever enough to hide his growing dejection. Life as a prisoner in an air-conditioned jail did not suit him. "Poor fellow," Madi said. "Just look at him! Young and strong and lovely… He needs grass to run on and things to chase and trees to pee against and air to breathe."

"I know, I know," Jonjo said. "So what do you suggest? We can't even let him be seen. And we can't let him live outside – he's not a sleigh dog, not a husky, he'd freeze. And what pleasure would it give him? Howling icy winds, snow underfoot to freeze his toenails off – "

Madi gazed at Bob. Now his exercise period was over, he had hidden himself in the cupboard. Soon the door would have to be closed on him. Prison cell. Meanwhile, to please Madi and Jonjo, he tried to appear interested in the bowl of food he had been given. He stared at it with dull eyes. Sometimes he even nibbled a scrap or two. "Good dog, Bob!" Jonjo said to him. "Eat up!" Bob gave his tail one and a half wags and buried his nose in the food. But he did not eat it.

"Look," Jonjo said to Madi, "this isn't any good. We're stuck. On our own, we can't do anything. We've got to get someone else involved, someone effective whom we can trust."

"Oh yes?" Madi said. "And who would that be? Not the beautiful Inge, by any chance?"

"Oh, shut up about Inge," Jonjo said.

But then Bob scrambled to his feet and made a frantic interruption.

"Bad!" he said. "Ung … Ing … Ing-errr … BAD!"

He showed his teeth and snarled.

"Well, that settles that!" Jonjo said. "Inge's out. Obviously Bob's met her and he hates her."

"How did he meet her? Why does he hate

her?" Madi said. "Oh well ... we're left with Max. At least we're sure that he's directly linked to Bob."

"But how's Inge mixed up in it?" Jonjo objected.

"Well, Max hates Inge, Bob hates Inge."

Jonjo said, "Hmm..." and shrugged. "So now what?" he said.

"Now we concentrate on Max. Use him to get out and scout around for a hiding place for Bob. Squeeze him till he pops his pips."

"Off you go, then," Jonjo said. "Give him the works."

Madi cornered Max. "I'm sorry we made you so angry the last time we talked," she said, staring earnestly at him with her large, dark, honest eyes.

"Oh, I was... I shouldn't have... I'm the one who's sorry."

"Then we're friends again?" Madi said, appealingly.

"Friends? Of course, yes," he said.

He wanted to escape. She did not let him. "Friends! Oh, good, super!" she beamed. "So may I ... could I ... ask you a big favour?"

"Well, it depends on —"

"You see," Madi said, "there's this Snomobile. The new one. And we – Jonjo and I – we've been in the old ones, and they're horrible. Noisy and smelly and windows you

31

can't see out of. But this new one … wow! It's
got lovely seats and everything. And we never
seem to get out of this place and we're not
allowed to drive because we're too young…"

"You want me to take you for a ride in the
new Snomobile, is that it? Well it's rather
difficult, you see — "

"But you can fix it, can't you? Oh, I knew
you could! Today, can you really take us for a
ride today? Three o'clock would be just
perfect. Oh, you are kind! I'll run and tell
Jonjo, three o'clock!"

She danced away merrily.

He walked away gloomily.

The new Snomobile was a smasher. The old
ones grumbled, the new one purred. The old
ones jostled you, the new one cradled you.

"And you can actually see out of the
windows!" Madi enthused. The old
Snomobiles had yellowing windows that
misted up.

Madi was ecstatic, Jonjo was excited. Max
was resigned. "Fasten your belts," he said.
"Properly."

"I've done mine!" cried Madi. "There! All
nice and tight!"

"Mine too," said Jonjo, snapping his seat-
belt.

The Snomobile vroomed, zoomed and
caroomed across crusted snow and hidden

32

depths of ice. It nosed smoothly through swirling grey-white drifts of powder snow, sending them scurrying. It rose on its cushion of air, wheezed gratefully and accelerated steadily, heading nowhere for a non-existent horizon.

"All right?" Max said glumly. Madi said, "Great!" and Jonjo said, "Super!"

"Where to?" Max said, minutes later.

"To a hiding place," Madi said sweetly.

"Sorry, didn't hear you," Max said.

"To a hiding place," Jonjo said, very distinctly.

"A hiding place? What do you mean, hiding place? Hiding place for what?"

"Bob," said Jonjo and Madi together.

"I don't get you," said Max. His voice had risen half an octave.

"Oh, yes you do," said Jonjo. "Bob, the dog. Good dog Bob. Your old four-footed friend."

"Let's stop," Madi suggested. "Stop anywhere. Then we'll have a little chat."

All her girlish sweetness was gone.

Max broke quickly.

"It was the rabbits," he confessed. "I couldn't stand the things they were doing to them. Obscene... They'd got them in plastic hutches, cramped up so that they couldn't move ... and their heads stuck out, just their heads ... and things on their brains, tubes stuck up their nostrils."

"Don't tell us any more," Madi said. "All done in the name of science..."

Max shrugged. "Well, it was a scientific institution. A major one."

"Who was the boss?" Madi demanded.

"As if we couldn't guess," said Jonjo.

"Well, yes – Dr Inge Lindstrom was in charge," Max said. "You could say she's in charge of *everything*. The whole OzTech operation. She just takes over..."

"Fancy that," said Madi. "Well, go on."

Max said, "At first, I pretended I wasn't seeing the things I was seeing. Or told myself that it was all very important, all for the good of humankind."

"But then you found out that it was all just experiments?" Jonjo suggested.

"Experiments for the sake of experiments," Max said. "Hideous, filthy things, being done for the sake of doing them."

"But there must have been some excuse, some reason!" Madi said.

"There was. Look, you know about the two major panics we've been through all these years since the 1980s –"

"The Greenhouse Effect and the holes in the Ozone Layer," Madi said. "How could anyone *not* know about them? New illnesses, new fuels to replace oil and petrol, new wars

34

between the Haves and Have-nots, new maps to show where the rising seas have eaten away the old coastlines –"

"You're mixing two things into one," Max said. "Well, why not? They're interconnected. But stick to our Hole in the Head, the one above us right now: and its effects on *our* animals and life forms."

Jonjo said, "Skin cancers and eye diseases from too much ultraviolet radiation. That sort of thing?"

"Yes. Those are some of the obvious ones. But there are also genetic changes. The *nature* of some animals seems to be changing. Our work concentrated on that."

"Why did you get involved?" Jonjo said. "You're a psychologist, not a – a genetic engineer."

"Just a psycho-ceramic," Madi said nastily.

"A what?" Max said.

"Psycho-ceramic. Crack-pot. Joke. Ha-ha."

"A joke, eh?" Max said wearily. "It's so old I'd forgotten it. Very funny."

"Seriously, what part did you play?" Jonjo said.

"If you change a sophisticated creature physically," Max said, "you also change it psychologically. If pigs could fly – if beef cattle could develop imaginations, a sense of possibilities – they might take a dislike to slaughterhouses. If sheep could communicate, talk, exchange ideas and information—"

"No more lamb chops and wool sweaters?"
Madi said.

"Probably not," said Max.

"What was Inge actually doing with her
rabbits and things?" Jonjo said.

"She – many people – had seen that UV
radiation was changing them. Causing
mutations. There seemed to be some super-
rabbits running around: rabbits that turned on
their predators, rabbits that had become too
cunning to be snared or shot. Above all,
rabbits that seemed able to communicate with
each other."

"Rabbits have always done that," Jonjo
said. "They show other rabbits their scuts,
their white tails, when there's danger about.
That's communicating."

"Not in words," Max said.

"You mean Inge had found rabbits that
talk? You're having us on!"

Max said, "I don't mean they talked as we
talk. They didn't say 'Good morning' or 'How
do you do' to each other. No more do donkeys
or dormice. Or dogs."

"'My doggie Pongo understands every word
I say, don't you, my love?'" Madi said,
imitating an old woman. "I suppose you're
right," she added, in her own voice. "Animals
do have languages. And often, we learn bits of
them. But talking *rabbits*…"

"Go on about Inge's experiments," Jonjo said. "She'd seen something new, right? And she started messing around with them, physically and mentally, right? – to see how far she could develop their new powers?"

"Exactly," Max said. He looked tired and guilty.

"And you helped?" Madi said.

"Yes. I devised tests, probed mental responses and capabilities. She kept breeding new strains – rabbits breed fast, which suited her purpose – and she applied my tests. I didn't help her in the laboratories but ... yes, I devised tests."

He rubbed his forehead. "I *enjoyed* devising the tests," he said. "Actually enjoyed it. Until I saw the animals in the laboratories."

There was a silence. Then Madi said, "What was her excuse for doing horrible things? She must have had an excuse!"

"Vanity," said Max instantly.

"What do you mean, vanity? Whose vanity?" Madi said. Then – "No, I think I can guess..."

"Dr Inge Lindstrom is a very vain woman," said Max. "She has a lot to be vain about. She is a success, a leader, a celebrity, an originator."

"And beautiful with it," Madi said.

"Yes, beautiful. Which means that she's newsworthy; which means that the very important subjects she genuinely knows about come before a huge public. TV, films, books, the lot. She *sells* science. Or her beauty does."

"And she's vain?"

"Vain, arrogant and greedy. She needs more and more success. Which all adds up to ... well, a wicked woman. The scientist's job is to understand how things work and hope to make them work better. Inge has gone beyond that. She wants to change things not for the better, but to please her own vanity."

"You mean she started behaving like God?" said Jonjo.

"Yes, or like Frankenstein. He made a monster. Inge went one better. She set up assembly lines of monsters."

"But the rabbits weren't monsters," Madi said. "I mean, they couldn't be, could they? Not rabbits."

"Suppose they were not rabbits, but rats!" Max said.

"What do you mean? All those stories about intelligent rats? But that's all hype, isn't it?"

"It's not all hype!" Jonjo said. "Remember that TV film? No, you wouldn't, you had flu and anyhow you were too young. But I remember the rats! Clusters of them in dark corners! They stared at you: stared and gibbered. All those eyes, staring! And raw tails! And greeny-yellow teeth!"

"Thank you, that's enough!" Madi said to Max. She was shuddering.

Jonjo said, "All right, I won't go on. But the thing was, there seemed to be *boss* rats. They sort of lectured the other rats, ordered them about. Even nipped at them. Aren't I right, Max?"

"You are right. But no one took much notice. All the talk was of rat plagues, rat infestation, how to get rid of rats. The important thing about them didn't make news. Well, not often. Did you watch TV in London, Jonjo?"

"That's about all we did," Jonjo said. "Madi was ill. We spent most of the time in our hotel room with the telly on."

"Did you see Inge on TV?"

"Mantrap Inge!" Madi said. "Yes, she was on quite often. False eyelashes and all."

"She doesn't wear false eyelashes," Jonjo said.

"Oh, sorry, a thousand pardons!"

"Why was she on TV?" Max said. "What did she talk about?"

"Well, rats," Jonjo said. "Yes, and new sorts of intelligence and communication. But it always seemed to start with rats, she was very close to them."

"She would be," Madi said.

Max said, "Rats communicating, obeying a leader, behaving like trained soldiers! Well, what comes next, do you think?"

"Rabbits?" Jonjo replied. "Yes, rabbits. Nice and gentle, easy to handle."

"And after rabbits?" Max said.

"Dogs?"

"Yes, dogs. Inge's greatest achievement was a dog. A particular dog."

"Bob!" Jonjo murmured. "Super-rats, super-rabbits, then a super-dog. But dogs don't behave like rats, they're not vicious."

"Bob's lovely, he's not a rat!" Madi cried.

Jonjo said nothing. Max said nothing.

"Bob's just a *dog*, he wouldn't hurt a fly!" Madi protested. "Would he?"

No reply.

Max ended the empty silence by standing up and saying, "Well, back to work."

Madi said, "Wait! You can't mean – you don't mean – that Bob's a *danger* to us! Because he isn't, he's just Bob!"

Max said, "Well, then there's nothing to worry about. Is there?"

Madi said, "Oh, yes there is! How come Bob was left to die in a MetrePak? Doesn't that worry you?"

Max ignored the question. He said, "We'll go for a ride in a Snomobile. Do some sightseeing, right? Get away for an hour or two."

DOWNFALL

There was no warning. They rode in the Snomobile for about a quarter of an hour. They stopped to look about. And then – the Snomobile's floor just sagged from under them. It dropped perhaps half a metre, tilting to one side so that everyone grabbed the arms of their seats.

"What the – ! What the – !" Max said. Madi gave a short yelp of terror.

Quite easily and smoothly, taking its time, the Snomobile began sinking through the snow and ice. It crunched its way down, making graunching noises as if it were eating the surface it rested on, chewing its way to its own burial.

And suddenly the windows showed sliding pictures of packed snow and ice, pictures that always moved up and up as the Snomobile went down and down. And still the Snomobile chewed its way downwards, tilting to this side then that, hanging on for long moments then uneasily letting its weight press down deeper still.

Jonjo found the interior-light buttons. Max, appalled, kept repeating "What the – ! What the – !" Madi screamed in earnest.

It seemed to take for ever for the Snomobile's descent to come to a definite end. But at last the fall was over; the Snomobile found a resting place. The cabin light beamed on three terrified faces. A little electronic voice kept saying, "OK to send, OK to send." Jonjo must have flicked the transmitter switch.

They looked about them. All but one of the windows were obscured by packed snow and ice. A pane of one double-glazed cabin window was missing. Heat from the cabin interior must have reached the single thickness of glass and warmed it: there was a soft thump as ice and snow fell away. They scrabbled across the tilted floor, pushing each other aside, to look through this window.

There was light. Dark, blue-grey light. And vague shapes close to and far away. Max muttered, "Thank God!" Jonjo said, "For what?" Max said, "We could have ended up in our coffin. Packed tight in snow and ice. But we haven't. There's space around us out there."

Madi said, "What happened? Did we fall through a crust?"

"That's it," Max said. "We broke through and fell into a ravine, or a cave, I don't know what. What do you think, Jonjo?"

Jonjo said, "We've got to get out. But can we? How many doors have we got? Three?"

"Three. The big loader door and the two crew doors."

"Shall I try them?"

"Might as well."

Jonjo pressed the loader-door button. There was the sound of electric motors spinning. Jonjo said, "Ah!" The motors tried harder, whined louder. Then there was a blue flash and all the lights went out.

They panicked, but only for a short time. Jonjo began opening and shutting things, blundering around in the blackness. "Got it!" he said at last: "Flashlight!" He switched on the big, powerful handlamp. By its light, Madi found another lamp. They were no longer in the dark.

"Where are we? How far from home?" Madi asked.

"Not far, we can't be," Max said. "I deliberately made sure of that." He was frowning over the Navplot. "Ah... I went round in a circle, you see, I didn't want to take any risks. Here we are." He poked his finger at the screen. The trace ended at a point near OzBase. "About 4,500 metres to go," he said.

"That's not far!" said Jonjo. "We could almost walk it."

"Not with the gear we're wearing. We wouldn't get half-way. Frozen stiff."

Madi said, "We don't have to walk, we just beep OzBase and they come and get us." Then she said "Oh...!" and looked frightened.

43

"*Oh!*" said Jonjo, imitating her. "*Oh* indeed. No electricity, no radio, no communications. Another thing: how do we get out?"

"Perhaps it's just fuses blown," Max said. "When we overloaded the door motors. Give me that torch."

Five strained and wordless minutes later, he called Jonjo and Madi over to the electrics section of the Snomobile and said in a grey voice, "Look."

Their eyes followed the beam of the handlamp to an inward bulge of snow and ice: to deformed sheet metal and twisted fingers of framework; and a jumble of junction boxes and control units. There were also wiring harnesses. The prettily coloured wires ran in ordered patterns till they reached the boxes. Then they splayed out like stale flowers in a vase, drooping this way and that. Wrenched out of the boxes.

"Aren't we the lucky ones," Max said, flatly and bitterly. "The one place where the bodywork got caved in had to be – precisely *here*." By the light of the lamp, his face looked twenty years older.

"You mean, the Snomobile's had its brains bashed in?" Jonjo said.

"That's what I mean."

"Well, you're the psychologist, the brain specialist!" Madi said and began giggling hysterically.

Jonjo put an arm round her shoulders. "Come on, Madi. It's all right, Madi, come on," he murmured.

"It's NOT all right, we're trapped and I HATE it here, you've got to get me OUT, please, PLEASE!"

As suddenly as she had started, she stopped. "Oh dear, listen to me!" she said primly and pecked a kiss at Jonjo's cheek. She even managed to control her shaking.

"What do we do now?" she said. "Any ideas?"

"The one thing we don't do," Max said, "is give up."

"That's right," Jonjo said. "We won't *die*. Where's the Snomobile handbook? Let's have a look. Good, great, here we are... Emergency Kits. That cupboard thing over there, Madi, next to the one with the red cross on it – open it up. Just push the knob, it should fall open... Goodness gracious *me*, imagine that, it actually does! Let's see what Santa Claus has brought us."

Santa Claus had been generous. They emptied the cupboard and arranged its contents in neat, distinct piles. If the batteries of the handlamps died, they did not want to thrash about in the dark trying to find things. But no one mentioned the possibility of the batteries failing...

"Four turtle doves, three French hens," Madi sang, as she sorted emergency food rations from the medical supplies.

"You're singing it all wrong, it goes 'Five gold rings, four calling birds, three French hens, two turtle doves —'"

"And a partridge in a pear tree!" Madi said triumphantly. She had found a bottle of brandy and placed the bottle in the very centre of the emptied cupboard.

It looked quite festive standing there in the glow of the handlamps, showing its elaborately printed labels.

But they could not get any of the three doors open.

They spent hours trying – first through the Snomobile's electrics, joining this wire to that socket, tracking this circuit to that fuse. "OK," Jonjo would say, as he gave a screw a final tightening. "Now try."

Madi, at the control console, said, "I press this button, right?"

"Yep. Give it a prod."

Three faces, carefully expressionless, avoided each other's gaze as Madi's finger descended. Then –

"*Pfzz!*"

A small blue flash.

Nothing else.

* * *

They tried brute strength. They removed a seat and undid the frame rails underneath. Meanwhile, Jonjo tried to force a door gap with a tyre lever. He managed to make a gap big enough to take the tips of two rails bolted together along their length to form a lever, a jemmy.

"Right, we're there," he said. They forced the jemmy into the gap. "OK ... one, two, three – PUSH!"

They pushed. The rails bent. The door stayed closed.

And all the time, it got colder and colder inside the Snomobile.

"Nothing to worry about," Max said. "We've got the three of us – three times 98.4 degrees Fahrenheit. Our combined body heat should be enough."

"And we've got this camping stove thing from the emergency packs," Madi said. "But we'll save that for cooking. Mustn't waste anything."

"I'm warm as anything, I'm actually sweating!" Jonjo said.

Through chattering teeth.

They made a good comical dinner from the mixture of emergency foods. The "Santa Claus" idea took hold: although it was nowhere near Christmas, they sang carols in the dark. They had decided to use the

47

handlamps only when necessary. They improvised beds from seat cushions. They were cheerful.

But it kept getting colder.

They slept huddled together with Max, the biggest, in the middle.

"You're our central-heating system," Madi said. Jonjo and Max dutifully said "Ha-ha."

But the cold bit deeper. Jonjo, awake, could not even rub his ice-block feet – his movements would wake the others. He lay rigid and miserable, trying not to think. What was there to think about? Only death by freezing. He could imagine the newspaper headlines...

BODIES OF TRAGIC THREE DISCOVERED
MUMMIFIED IN ICY TOMB

JONJO'S GALLANT LAST HOURS
IN FROZEN HELL

'SNO USE – ALL DEAD!

Good, that last one, Jonjo thought. Snappy. Cold-snap snappy. How would the story go on?

Dr Max Gibbon, always a chilly personality, was at his chilliest today...

Jonjo's last message, scribbled with icy fingers soon to be stilled by the chill presence of Death...

48

He enjoyed these mental exercises enough to forget his discomfort. Perhaps he would one day be an ace reporter?

More likely, an ice block.

He slept and dreamed of a town, a city. Where was it? Somewhere high up on the world map, near the Hole in the Head.

He was with a wind-farmer, a big gingery man with thick golden hairs on his strong red arms. The man's accent kept changing. Sometimes he sounded Dutch, sometimes English, sometimes like a Texan in an American film. He was pleasant enough at first, but he wouldn't stop talking.

"Ach, ja!" he boomed. "I am still a farmer, ho yuss! But now I farm the wind not the soil. In wind is money, plenty gelt for the honest farmer!"

Jonjo thought, "Honest farmer...! Big windbag, more like!" All the same, he was impressed by what the wind-farmer pointed out to him: endless fields of windmills, great tapered metallic spires topped by slowly rotating, slender propeller blades. The thousands of blades sang a song. It was both high and low. There was an underlying deep bass thrum, but also a thready, high, whirring whistle.

"Used to be wheat, kid, all wheat," the wind-farmer said, suddenly turning American.

49

"But I said to myself, 'Get out of wheat and into wind. Out of vitamins and into voltages!' Best advice I ever had!"

"I know about wind-farming," Jonjo muttered. He was growing sick of the man's self-satisfaction. "Everyone knows."

"Sun and air," the man said. "Look you, boyo, there's sunshine for you!" (Now he had a Welsh accent.) The man swept his heavy arm to point at a great field of glass-fronted solar panels. It hurt Jonjo's eyes to look at them. The panels formed endless arrays of what might have been chicken houses, but the structures glittered savagely. "Sunny money, sonny!" the man – American again – boasted. "Megabucks all the way!"

"I know about solar-electrics," Jonjo said. "Solar panels pick up the heat from the sun and convert it into electricity —"

"Megabucks, bobbing ducks!" the man boomed. And all at once Jonjo was looking at a line of duck-like plastic toys connected by a wire running through their middles. The ducks bobbed on wavelets. The wind and solar farms were gone. They were by the seashore, standing up to their ankles in freezing water. The ducks stretched all along the coastline. They never stopped bobbing. They were quite pretty, but only plastic. Not alive.

"Wanna know something?" the man said. "Ducks make bucks."

"You don't have to explain!" Jonjo said, almost shouting. The sea was so cold that his feet and ankles were agony. "*I* know, *everybody* knows, about wind and solar and tidal power stations! Energy from *renewable sources*, right? It's been going on for years! Ever since the turn of the century! Tell me something new!"

"You want to mind your manners, sonny," the man threatened.

A single duck bobbed up from the water. It had circular eyes like a target and painted feathers. It squeaked, "I've just laid a microvolt! Not an egg, an erg!"

Jonjo said, "I know, I *know*. Everyone knows."

He was furious. He felt as if he were a tiny tot at his first school being taught about things that he already knew: about smog and CO_2, pollution, dying forests, dead lakes, oil wars, the disappearance of petrol cars –

"I know, I know, I KNOW!" he shouted at the duck.

The man said, "Now see here, son, you button your lip or I'll tan your hide." He pushed his enormous face into Jonjo's, blacking out the sky.

The bobbing duck was angry too. It jumped from the water and jabbed its beak at Jonjo's ankles. The wire running through its body held it back. And in any case, Jonjo only had to move his feet –

But he couldn't! They were frozen to the shore! And the duck's beak was snapping and hacking at his ankles, hurting him horribly –

And the man had lifted his big arm, it was high in the air, it would come down and smash him! –

Then a voice said, "You all right in there? You OK? Come on, wake up...! You OK?"

The rescue party had arrived.

WISHING WELL

Madi, Max and Jonjo clambered out of their bed. Max looked blue-grey and ill. Madi was shivering and dazed. Jonjo's feet were agony. "The duck pecked me," he said.

"What?" said the leader of the rescuers.

"Nothing," Jonjo said. He rubbed the pain out of his legs and the dream out of his mind. "How did you get to us?" he asked. "We tried and tried, but we couldn't get a door open. Or the electrics working." Then he noticed that the lights were on, the fan heaters blowing warm air, the console lights shining.

"There's a sort of master switch that brings in an over-ride supply," the man explained. "It's in the manual, actually, under 'Master Switch'. Don't know how you missed it." He sounded embarrassed. Jonjo knew he was trying not to say, "How could you have been so stupid?"

Max said, "Fool! Moron!" He was looking at the manual and accusing himself. Madi said, "We all missed it, all three of us. It's all right, Max."

Jonjo said, "We were scared. Thought we'd never get out. Thought we'd die here."

The rescuer said jokingly, "Oh, we couldn't allow that! Snomobiles cost money!"

Max and Jonjo saw just how stupid they had been. Of course the Snomobile would be missed, and the people in it. Of course they and their vehicle were tagged at Control. Of course it was the easiest thing in the world to track them and rescue them.

Madi was thinking of something else. "How quickly can you get us back to OzBase?" she said.

"Quick as a flash. But what's the hurry? How about coffee and something to eat first?"

"No, I want to get back now, I must get back," she said. To Jonjo she murmured, "*Bob*." He nodded to her. "You go back now, we'll be there soon," he said. He wanted to find out where they were. The knowledge might be useful.

They took Madi away in a little Snowster runabout. To reach it, they had to climb rope ladders. The Snomobile was buried so deep that only its roof aerials showed.

"Coffee, then," their rescuers said when the noise of the Snowster's motors had faded. The Snomobile's cabin grew warmer and warmer. The coffee was scalding hot and delicious. Jonjo enjoyed it.

Max, ashamed of himself, stayed gloomily silent.

Bob greeted Madi with ecstatic wrigglings and whimpers. She clasped him to her, weeping.

He cried too, from his mouth, soaking her shoulder. He put his front legs round her neck and made her still wetter with lickings. She didn't care. "Oh, Bob! Poor Bob! Did you think we'd forgotten you?" she said. "We couldn't forget you, not ever!"

"Good dog Bob," he answered and licked so hard at her face that she thought her nose would be pulled off.

There were six men in the rescue team. Two of the team had gone with Madi. They looked like great fat dolls in their multi-layered suits and eye-goggled head gear. Jonjo knew the four remaining – Karl, "Smithy", Giancarlo and Dr Stepan. Karl was in charge.

"I'm not in a hurry if you're not," he said. "I want to look around. See exactly what happened." Jonjo joined the men.

They reconnected wires and pressed buttons. Doors that should have opened hours earlier whirred open now, at a touch. Max did not look up. He hunched in the Snomobile letting his coffee get cold.

One opened door showed a wall of snow and ice. Jonjo kicked at the wall. "Solid," he said. Giancarlo gave it a kick for luck. There was a tumbling rumble – and the wall fell away. It became an untidy, glittering heap. Beyond it there was almost, but not quite, darkness. They shone their lamps into it.

55

"It's a ... damnbig ... great strong ... *cave*!" Karl said. He was a Finn, huge and competent. And he was right: the cave was very big. It got bigger as they entered it, their lamps picking out glistening icy walls that seemed to come alive as light awakened them. "Whee-ooo!" Karl shouted. Giancarlo gave a whistle of amazement.

"Quiet!" Dr Stepan said. "We've got a million tonnes over our heads! If it collapses..."

"It won't," said Smithy. "Everything slopes downhill. The Snomobile fell through the roof at the only weak spot, near the surface. Chance in a million. We're safe here. Safer than houses."

They flashed their lamps upwards at strong arches and cathedral vaults that formed domes high above their heads. "It would take something to shift that lot," Smithy said. His voice was awed.

"And how many million years to create it?" said Karl.

Smithy found the Wishing Well. It was like a great dimple in the icy floor of the cave; or a huge plug-hole; or a vast dew pond. "My God!" he whispered. All of them spoke quietly now, awed by the vastness and silence of the cave. "My God, what caused *that*?"

Karl said, "Volcano, you know? Could be

subterranean volcano, you think? Once upon a time?"

"There's water in it," Smithy said. "Well, ice, anyhow. Right up to the brim. It must have been water ages ago..."

"A spring," Giancarlo said, trying out the word. "You call it that? A geyser? But long ago, so long ago."

The five of them stood staring at it. Smithy groped inside the layers of his clothing and found a coin. He threw it on the flat, almost black surface of the frozen water. "I wish, I wish," he muttered. Then – "Wishing Well, tell me true, what am I to make of you?" There was some hushed laughter. The coin tinkled and skidded, then settled on the surface. They shone their lights at it. It looked very small.

As they watched, an astonishing thing happened. The coin tilted very slightly: then sank. Not far, perhaps a millimetre or two. But it sank, definitely, then settled. Its bright outline was blurred.

"But it couldn't!" Smithy muttered. "Not in this cold! Unless the heat of my body – the coin was warm...?"

They stood staring for some time, then began making their way back to the Snomobile. At first they were silent. Then Jonjo started humming the Snow White song, *I'm wishing, I'm wishing, for the one I love.* The others picked up the tune. Karl sang it in a hideous falsetto. And suddenly they were the Seven Dwarfs. *Heigh ho! Heigh ho! It's off to work we go!* They capered about like fools until Karl said, "Nearly there. Better behave ourselves."

Dr Stepan, a mineralogist, said, "Ah yes, we must consider Max. The sad doctor Max, our *psychologist*. Tell me, someone, why do we need a *psychologist* in these latitudes?"

"Because only mad men would come here!" said Karl.

"Perhaps it's something to do with the Hole in the Head," Jonjo said, cheekily. "His own head, maybe?"

They laughed. Jonjo soon stopped. He felt ashamed of mocking Max. Max wasn't all that bad.

But when they reached the Snomobile, Max didn't look too good. He was as they had left him, crouched on a seat. And still he had not drunk his coffee.

Twenty-four hours later, Jonjo told Madi, "I've found it!"

"Found what?"

"The perfect boarding kennel!"

"What are you on about?"

"Kennel for Bob, of course. Somewhere for him to live. A proper place, with room to run about, and a snug place to sleep – the lot!"

"I don't believe you."

58

"Just listen. The Snomobile, remember? Buried in the ice?"

"Don't be wet – of course I remember."

"Well, that's it. Bob's new home!"

"Oh, great, terrific. We get him there somehow, with nobody noticing, then leave him there alone, to freeze to death."

"No, listen. I've made friends with the rescue men. They think I'm all right. They let me drive them back in the Snowster *and* they said I can use it whenever I like, providing I follow all the Safety Regs."

"So we can take Bob to the Snomobile?"

"And visit him every day! You know, visit him, stay with him, then come back. And all legit!" Madi's face became radiant. "I love you, Jonjo! You're my favourite brother!"

"Stop messing me about. It's all fixed. Control knows we won't do anything silly with the Snowster. Anyhow, they'll keep us tagged. If anything went wrong, we'd either return to base or stay in the Snomobile. It's got heating, lighting, the lot."

"But if the batteries run flat?"

"Oh, that's all taken care of. You just press buttons and one motor starts and that charges the batteries within twenty minutes. It's so simple that *Bob* could do it!"

"Oh, poor darling Bob —"

"Never mind the slop, just think how perfect everything is. We ferry him out, leave him, drive around in the Snowster making it quite clear that we're enjoying ourselves – you know, fancy turns and all that —"

"But all the time we're looking after Bob! And he's got room to run about —"

"He's got a whole huge enormous cave, complete with Wishing Well and every mod con. Then he curls up and goes bye-byes in his luxury residence. And nobody suspects anything!"

"Oh, Jonjo, my clever lovely brudderkins!"

"Stop messing me about. And I wish you'd cut out the twentieth-century gush. You get it from those crummy old films on the viddy. You imitate them. You sound a real berk."

"'Berk' is a twentieth-century word. So boo-sucks."

"Boo-sucks…! You're pathetic!"

"Boo-sucks and no returns. Anyhow, who cares? All I care about is Bob."

Max, frozen with guilt, took a long time to thaw out.

"I've been trying to cheer him up. In the lounge," Madi told Jonjo. "But it didn't work."

"As if I cared," Jonjo said. "Let him stay worried. We've never got him to tell us the whole Bob story, have we? We still don't know why Bob was dumped here."

"Mantrap Inge," Madi said. "You can bet it's all down to her."

"You would say that."

"I know I'm right. And so do you. It's her. I feel it in my bones."

"Bones!" said Jonjo. "I got two big ones from that cook, the skinny one. Told him I was taking up Eskimo art, carving things in bone, ha-ha."

"Bones for Bob? Terrific! Let's take them to him right now!"

"Not till after three. All the Snowsters are out."

"*Bones!* I can't wait to see Bob's face!"

They got their Snowster at about four – not that time made much difference, you always seemed to need to use the Snowster's headlamps, which stuck out like frogs' eyes from the bubble-car bodywork.

They squabbled about who would drive; then settled themselves on the heated seats, fastened their belts and tucked Bob between them. The motors went "Whrrr – phweeee!"

You checked fuel/power status, communications, Panic Pack and a few other essentials. Then – "Phweeee... weepeepeep!" and you were off, cutting twin swathes through the snow crust, sending up frosty clouds in your wake, feeling the soggy but sure lurches of the suspension, making wide, unnecessary, sweeping curves for the hell of it.

"Not so fast, they'll see!" Madi shouted to

Jonjo. He was driving. He grunted but slowed down. She was right. Someone would be watching them through binoculars, tracking them with electronic bugs. Better behave.

It was a short trip – too short – to the sunken Snomobile.

Before the Snowster had completely stopped, Madi tumbled out of it and began running, clutching her share of the bones. ("Half each!" Jonjo had said. "No favouritism!") Bob rushed ahead, and back again, and ahead again. Before she had thrown down the Snomobile's rope ladder and started climbing down it, Bob was already inside welcoming them. They heard his carefully muted barking and the scrabble of his feet.

Then he was jumping at them, strangling them with his legs round their necks, licking, rolling, charging, wriggling, wagging, falling over himself…

"Bob, Bob, silly lovely Bob!" Madi said, throwing herself down on the floor so that Bob could rush at her and pretend to pull her to pieces.

"Bob, look! – bones!" Jonjo said, tearing the wrapping from his present. "For you, Bob!"

At first Bob was too busy to notice the bones. But when at last he stopped saying "Bob good dog!" and tying himself in knots, he picked up one bone and held it in his mouth like a white moustache. He stared gravely from Madi to Jonjo, slowly wagging his tail, then he said "Oof!" and threw the bone high in the air.

That started it. Madi and Jonjo chased Bob through the Snomobile, out into the cave, round and round the Wishing Well. Bob threw his bones in the air – bounced them off glistening walls of ice – made brilliant escapes just when Jonjo or Madi thought they'd cornered him.

When all three were exhausted, Bob settled down between Jonjo and Madi and gave the bones a serious gnawing while Madi played with the ruff of fur round his neck.

Later, they tried to teach him more words. He could understand what was wanted but found it hard to force out the right sounds. It was slow but happy work.

And there was another new face at OzBase: their mother's.

She had not changed. She was not the sort to change. She would always move fast, speak briskly, throw penetrating glances from her large, dark eyes. She would always, presumably, have a small, tight waist, neat hands with short-nailed, efficient fingers, the sort of hair that didn't need hairdressers – she could snip it herself into a springy, dark helmet that fitted perfectly.

"Time we took a holiday," she said, as soon as the quick, firm volley of kisses and greetings was over. "I've missed you. You've missed me. We'll whizz off somewhere and have a good time together, right?"

"Great!" Jonjo said. "Marvellous!" said Madi. But almost at once, their smiles faded and they exchanged sideways looks. Madi's lips formed the word "Bob". Bob could not be left. Madi and Jonjo could not both go on holiday. One had to stay behind.

Madi sorted it out with a series of complicated fibs about why she did not want to leave OzBase just now. She knew that her mother would not bother to listen. She would say, "Yes, understood. You stay on and I'll take you on holiday later when you've finished with everything here." Which was what her mother did say.

So Madi waved her brother and mother goodbye as they got into the chopper that would carry them to Oslo *en route* for England. As she waved, she wondered. She wondered if she would grow up to be like her taut, neat, able, successful mother – did she want to become like that? She wondered about her lanky, tousled, clever, ineffective father – where was he now, what was he doing, did he miss his family?

But then she thought of Bob and forgot everything else.

AHDI UM BOB!

At first, the OzBase people were uneasy about Madi going out alone in the Snowster. But within days, they got used to it. She grinned as she put on her multi-layered gear, smiled as she efficiently ran through the Checkout procedures, waved as she whooshed off with a cheerful farewell flurry of ice and snow.

"Good kid, she's beeping us," they said in Control.

"Good kid, she really knows how to handle a Snowster," they said.

"That Madi, she's a good kid," they all agreed as she and her Snowster faded into grey-white nothingness.

The good kid was cunning. Each trip she made followed a different course – to begin with. But in the end, every trip led to the buried Snomobile, and Bob.

"Good kid, she's checking in regular as clockwork!" they said, back at OzBase. They weren't to know that Madi had pre-recorded her Commset and bleeper – left them lying in the snow, well away from her invariable destination, the Snomobile. She did not want them to know. Bob was her joyous secret, not to be shared with anyone; because anyone might turn out to be Bob's enemy.

So her bleeper bleeped at the stated intervals, and her Commset regularly carried her voice to OzBase – "Madi, speaking, Madi here, all OK, all OK, no more from me for sixty minutes, all OK, Madi over and out." Sometimes her voice was live: usually it was pre-recorded. But it was always there, on time.

Which meant that she could spend hour after hour with Bob.

When his first ecstasies were over – the wild charges, the pretended attacks with the snapping fangs, the rough-and-tumble wrestling matches – when Bob had finished with these, he stretched himself on the floor beside Madi and rested his chin on her thigh. In this position – for she lay on the floor too, her head raised on cushions – he could gaze into her eyes and adore her; and she could play with his ears or stroke the soft, silky dome of his head and hold long conversations with him.

"Oh yes, you're a fine fellow, aren't you, Bob?"

"Bob good dog."

"But your ears need combing. I mean, look at these knots here! And here!" (She pulls his ears: he clamps his white teeth on her hand, pretending to be angry. He says "Grrr!" in his throat, but his tail wags.)

66

"How do you keep your teeth so clean, Bob? Have you got a toothbrush hidden somewhere?"

Bob does not understand. He falls back on his favourite phrase, "Bob good dog."

"Shall we have an English lesson now?" she says. "You really should learn some more words. I mean, you're so handsome and intelligent and lovely, aren't you? But lazy, Bob. You're a lazy devil, you are, you know you are!"

She tugs at his ears. He makes terrifying snaps with his jaws – *glop! glop!* – and rolls his eyes fiercely. All the time, his tail wags in a leisurely way and his eyes stare into hers, doting on her.

Then he surprises her. "Uh-morrer uh-gain," he says, with an effort that nearly chokes him. "Uh-morrer, Ahdi um Bob!"

Madi's brain spins – first with amazement, then with the effort to translate. "Tomorrow?" she says. "Is that what you mean?"

"Uh-morrer uh-gain."

"Oh, you clever thing! Yes, 'Tomorrow again'! I promise!"

"Uh-morrer, Ahdi um Bob."

"Yes, tomorrow I come to see you. Aren't you *brilliant*?" She kisses him. She thinks, Those are the last words I say to him when I leave him. And he's learned them!

* * *

67

Now she teaches Bob more earnestly and seriously than ever before. For ten minutes, he does very well.

"Ay-boo!" he says when she says "Table".

He even manages "Oh-oh-bee!" for "Snomobile", and "Ight" for "Light".

Then for a second time, he amazes her. To show him what she means by "light", Madi switches a lamp on and off. The switch is a flat tab set in the wall, designed to be operated by heavily gloved, clumsy hands or even by an elbow.

Bob suddenly jumps up, stretches upwards to his full height – and prods the switch with his nose. The light comes on.

"Ight!" Bob tells Madi, his whole body wriggling in triumph. "Bob ight! Bob unnit!"

"Oh, Bob, that's wonderful!" Madi says, wide-eyed with delight. "Bob done it! The light!"

Bob has not finished. Again he reaches up on his hind legs. Again he dabs the switch with his nose. "Ight gong!" he says. "Bob unnit!"

"Yes, it's gone, the light's gone, and you did it! You're the cleverest dog in the world!"

Yet ten minutes later, he has almost forgotten his triumph, or lost interest in it. Now he wants to take Madi for a walk.

"But Bob, let's do more English lessons first!"

No. She is to walk with him. "Come this

way," he tells her with his tossing head: "Come on, no time to waste."

"Well, at least say 'Walk'. Go on, Bob, say it: 'Walk'."

"Awk," he mutters, uninterestedly. Then he leads her into the cave.

She thought Bob wanted to show her the Wishing Well – a place he liked. The ground was littered with thoroughly cleaned, meatless bones. So, when they reached it, Madi said, "Oh yes, great! The Wishing Well. Here are all your bones. Say 'Bones', Bob. Go on, say it!"

But he refused. He ran round her twice, then led her onwards, into the deeper, narrower darknesses. She had to bend double. Bob ran ahead, often turning to make sure she was following. His eyes glowed in the beam of her handlamp and the white bits of his furry coat seemed to stand out separately. "Spooky," she said to herself as the curved frozen walls closed in on her. She was not really afraid – just uneasy when Bob disappeared from view, or when the echoes of his pattering pads suggested scuttling creatures.

Then he started barking. She could not see him, he was a long way ahead. His barking was high-pitched. She recognized the tone of it: it meant, "This is it, this is what I want you to see." But she could not go to him, the walls ahead formed a tunnel too small for her. Bob couldn't or wouldn't understand: he kept insisting she should come and see.

At last he came out of the tunnel and stood in front of Madi, looking into her eyes and making small urgent whooping noises in his throat. "Bob," she said to him, taking his front paws, "Bob, you must *tell* me. Speak to me and *tell* me."

"Bob good dog," he said uncertainly.

"No, Bob, don't be so lazy. What is in there?" She nodded her head at the cave. "Say it, Bob, *say it*."

He could not.

"Is it bad, Bob?"

"Woh. Woh." That meant No.

"Is it good, Bob?"

"Good, ye-ap, good." (Ye-ap was as near as Bob could get to Yes.)

"Is it like you or me, Bob? Does it walk, talk, move?" She made a "dog" with her hand and fingers, then a "man" with two fingers. She "walked" these figures.

Bob understood. "Woh. Buh ... buh ... buh..." He meant, No – but, but, but... Madi said, "You mean, it's alive?"

"Ye-ap!"

Then Bob did strange things. He lowered his nose to the ground; stared fixedly ahead of himself; raised his head, until his nose pointed on high; finally he jumped into the air, snapped his jaws and sat down, proudly. His tongue lolled from his grinning mouth and his tail wagged.

"Something you caught, Bob? Something that flies? Like a bird?" Madi made a bird with both her hands and flapped its wings.

Bob's tail stopped wagging. He looked at her sorrowfully.

"Woh," he said.

"Well, what was it like, Bob? Try and tell me, do try!"

He thought about this for some time. At last he came to her and showed that he wanted his muzzle held in her hands. Madi obeyed. "Is this right? Bob?"

"Ye-ap."

"Go on, then," Madi said.

Now Bob did a still stranger thing. Concentrating hard, he licked his lips round his mouth for many seconds. When his mouth was so wet that his lips dripped saliva, he carefully blew a wet spit bubble into Madi's hands.

"Oh! You disgusting dog!" she cried, snatching her hands away.

"Bob good dog! Good dog, Bob!" he said. His eyes showed how deeply hurt he was. Madi was at once sorry.

"Woh 'gusting, Bob good dog!" he said.

Madi was too confused to answer him in words. So many things had happened in the last seconds. First – this must be the explanation – Bob had made a picture for her, in the form of a bubble of spit. Second, he had at once caught on to a new, long word – "Disgusting". Third, he had thrown the word straight back to her.

"Lovely Bob!" she said putting her arm round his neck. "You're getting cleverer every minute. Now, listen. You saw a round thing, a bubble-shaped thing, in there. Right?"

"Ye-ap. Losser. *Losser.*"

"There are *lots* of round things?"

"Ye-ap. Ye-ap!"

"And you jump up, like this, and catch them?"

"Ye-ap! Bob good dog! 'Atch losser!"

On her wrist, Madi's personal bleeper sounded. "Time's up, Bob. Just when we were getting somewhere... Bob, I've got to leave you."

The dog's tail went down.

"Uh-morrer uh-gain?" he said, sadly.

"Tomorrow again. I promise, Bob. I swear."

As she got into her Snowster, she heard his voice come up to her from his Snomobile home. "Uh-morrer!" it said, very sadly.

BUNNIES AND BOW-WOWS

Back at OzBase, Madi knew straight away that something odd was happening in the lounge. It was full of people, all silent.

But the lounge was never silent when there were people in it. Everyone was off duty, everyone talked and laughed. This silence was strange.

She gently pushed the door open and entered. Each person held a drink, but no one was drinking.

In the very centre of the room, flamingly colourful and somehow oversized, stood Dr Inge Lindstrom. Even through the perfect make-up, Madi could see the flush of fury on her cheeks. Her eyes seemed to throw blue fire.

"You want some trouble, little man?" she shouted. "All right, you know, I give it you. Much trouble!" She flung each word from her like a dagger.

"Cool it, Inge," someone muttered. "Let's not spoil —"

Inge did not listen.

"You were always a silly little man, a weakling, that is your word, right?" She pronounced it as "veekling". It sounded even worse that way. "A weakling, a *runt*!" she added. She said it "rrrundt". She made a garbage sack of the word.

Madi wasn't tall enough to see who Inge was attacking. She knew who it was when a small man stood up and, without a word, blundered towards the door. It was Max. His face was blotched scarlet, his lips twitched and his eyes stared. At the door, he collided blindly with Madi, stopped, and turned and faced Inge. "You blas– you blasted – you damned —"

She did not let him finish. "Enough, you've opened your mouth enough!" she screeched. "Enough for today, enough for all time! GET OUT!"

Madi went with Max. He was so shaken that she almost steered his footsteps. She took him to her room and sat him in a little chair. She got him a glass of water and watched it jiggle in his shaking hand.

She said, "What was all that about?"

At first Max would say nothing. Then he would not stop talking.

"That *bitch*," he began, "I wish someone would kill her. Me, *I*'d like to kill her! But I haven't the nerve. A weakling, a runt..."

"Never mind that," Madi said. "What was it all *about*?"

"Rabbits and dogs," Max said. He attempted a laugh. "Bunnies and bow-wows."

Madi's mind flashed an image of Bob. She leaned forward. "About Bob," she said, "you've got to tell me some time. Tell me now."

"Bob..." he said. "Yes, it ended with Bob. Before that it was rats and rabbits. And monkeys and pigs and cats. We never got anywhere with the cats – well, I never thought we would, they're a race apart — "

"That was when you were trying to teach them things, right?"

"Yes, teach them things. Because they seemed to be becoming *teachable*. But I've told you about it."

"Yes. Inge wanted to explore all the changes, possibly make use of some of them — "

"Make use of them? You could put it that way. What she had in mind was a huge statue of Dr Inge Lindstrom, All-Time Genius, Creator of new life forms, new kinds of intelligence, a whole new style of life for this planet!"

"By breeding animals that became intelligent servants for humans? But that wouldn't work, that's stupid."

"*Is* it?" Max was coming to himself. He had stopped shaking. "Are you sure it's stupid? What creatures *don't* we use at this very moment?"

"I know we eat sheep and cattle and fish and all that, but that's different."

"You're missing the point. Think of ... oh, think of elephants in Sri Lanka. They handle trees better than any tractor. Think of police and security and drug-detecting dogs – of horses working as teams, dray horses, milk-float horses, the ploughman's team —"

"Yes, I suppose you're right. I'm too young to have seen those things. All the same —"

"Each cow goes to its own stall for milking. It doesn't have to be told. The old-time dray horses – each horse knew how to back up a little bit here and another bit there to start the barrel rolling, help the drayman do his work. As for elephants —"

"All right, I've got it. What did Inge want?"

"Surely you can see?" Max said, wearily. "Have you never heard of the Babes in the Wood? They went to sleep, didn't they, and the nice kind birdies came and covered them with leaves."

"But that was a fairy story!"

"But suppose you could make it come true? Suppose you could teach and command the birds – and make them understand what you want – then if they would actually do it! Think of whole *races* of animals, all able to understand propositions, all able to communicate with us and with each other, all co-operating to do what you want them to do!"

"I still think it's nonsense. The animals simply wouldn't play."

"Name one species that wouldn't..."

"Cats. You said so yourself. They won't obey."

"You've never heard of circuses? They had them even in the twentieth century. Performing lions and tigers. If you've got whips, drugs, blank cartridges and electric probes, even the big cats learn to obey."

"I don't want to hear."

"No more do I. Not now. But in the beginning with Inge, it was all fascinating. Oh yes, I fell for it. And her."

"And then you saw the light?"

"No, the dark. Gathering darkness. So I told Inge I couldn't take any more, I'd quit. No, that's not the truth, I said I'd *have* to quit, I really *would* quit, I'd take up a job at OzBase or something... I didn't have the guts to quit there and then. I went blah blah blah."

"You still haven't told me what happened just now in the lounge. Why was Inge yelling at you?"

"Someone asked her about progress with Animal Intelligence, and she smiled – oh, she was so quiet and modest! – and she began talking about her progress communicating with rabbits. And I could *see* the rabbits, and the cages ... and she was being so *modest* ... and someone said, 'You seem to be on the right track' and I found myself shouting out, 'For God's sake, the *right* track, are you mad?' And I couldn't stop, I said too much too loudly. I

77

think I even threatened her with exposure – telling the world about the dangers of her work. And she turned on me. She smashed me. That was when you came in." He shrugged.

Then Madi said, "Tell me about Bob."

He drew a deep breath and told her. His words became pictures in Madi's mind...

It had happened like this.

Max had let Inge know that he wanted to leave, he could not stomach any more, it was all too much.

"Then quit! Leave! Go!" she spat at him.

"Look, I don't want us to part on bad terms, but you must understand my moral position –"

"Your *moral* position! Jellyfish, woodlice, toads! – so creatures like you have *moral* positions, do they?"

"Please, Inge..."

"*Your* moral position! Oh, it must be very special, your moral position! I have no moral position, of course – no anxieties, no doubts, no, none at all! Very well. But while you play games with moral positions, what do you think I am playing? Not your easy psychological stuff, your games with worry-beads... No, little man, I play *physical* games, the games that matter! With *this*, and *this*, and *this*!"

She picked up a scalpel, a needled syringe, a surgical clamp and threw them at him. The scalpel stuck quivering in the door behind him.

"Please, Inge, please listen!"

"Not Inge, not to you. You shall learn to address your superiors properly. I am your superior every way, yes? So Dr Lindstrom, address me so! That is how you talk to your superior who is also your boss!"

"Dr Lindstrom, just let me explain!"

"No more, no more, we are finish, go to OzBase, go to hell."

Max sweated, trembled and could say nothing. Inge flung instruments into stainless-steel sinks, knocked over a stool, muttered under her breath. Her startling eyes were charged with blue lightning.

The dog Bob, feeling the thunder in the air, sidled up to Max, wagging his tail uncertainly, licking Max's hand. Max knew Bob. He had noticed the dog half a dozen times before – admired his handsomeness, liked his friendliness. Now Max stroked Bob's head, having nothing better to do with his hands.

"If you are going, GO!" Inge shouted. "And take your flabby hands off my livestock!"

"Your *livestock*?" Max blurted. "A fine animal like this – he's just livestock?"

"Just livestock," Inge said. When she spoke, Bob cowered closer to Max. "Just livestock, just another of hundreds of animals, thousands of anxieties and problems. The dog's cage is over there. Tomorrow, I

79

continue his treatment."

Bob whined. Max stared at the dog and at Inge. He said, "You can't. You musn't."

"Oh! So now my jellyfish man becomes bold! He gives orders! Dr Lindstrom must not play her games with *this* pretty dog, the great man is saying 'no'! Is that it?"

"I am merely saying – look, surely you cannot — "

"Very well, I cannot, I shall not. The great man must be obeyed. Here is my present to you: the dog. He is yours, I give him to you, take him!"

Max found the courage to say, "Agreed. I will take him. Anything rather than see him — "

"Take him, take him!" Inge said. "And also," she added, "take some good advice. *Get rid of him. Fast.*"

Max said, "No. He is going to live."

"Is he, now?" Inge said, bitter-sweetly. "*Even though he's third stage?*"

"He's third stage?" Max echoed, hollowly. "That is monstrous! You can't mean it!"

"Yes, I do. Stage one, stage two, stage three. He's come through them all. Very successfully – largely thanks to you, my little man, for animals have psyches, yes? And you have been so helpful in manipulating their minds, yes?"

"At least I never did the things you do," Max began.

"Oh, how true! The little man never

handled a scalpel, never dirtied his hands! But this animal's mind and body are now at stage three. He is ... *adjusted*, physically and mentally."

"That's almost like calling him a monster!"

"A monster, if you like. But remember one thing, little man. He is your monster as much as mine! You helped created him!"

"I had no intention of —"

"You worked to make him. Now I am telling you to work to destroy him."

"But look, Inge —"

"Dr Lindstrom is my name. Goodbye, little man, goodbye, little doggie. Oh, and a last word, my brave psychologist..."

"What?"

"*Slay the monster!*"

Another humiliation for Max followed. Vague as his plans were, miserable and confused as the outlook was, he had to entrust the practical details to Inge. For she alone had the authority to arrange matters.

It took her just a day. "You go to OzBase on Wednesday," said her voice over the telephone.

"But that leaves me only two days to see to everything!"

"So, see to everything in two days."

"But... I've been trying to think things out ... I don't see how I can do what needs to be done *here*, if you see what I mean... The problem of disposal and everything..."

"Ah, so my little man wants great oceans and forests, or frozen wastes, in which to hide a body. Is that it?"

"Yes, because, you see, I was thinking..."

Certainly he had been thinking; thinking until his brain reeled.

1. The dog Bob must die. No disputing that. He and all such creatures could not be allowed to survive.

2. How to kill him? With his bare hands? You must be joking. With poison? – but which poison? And if the poisoned body were discovered, and the poisoner traced...

3. And even if it were not discovered, how could the body be safely disposed of? Did it – or did it not – contain its own genetic "poisons"? Could the dead body pass on its dangers?

4. An axe, a sealed suitcase, throw it out of the chopper... Absurd. The other people in the chopper would see.

5. Drug the dog, pack him up, dispose of him in the snow-and-ice wilderness surrounding OzBase.

Then Inge Lindstrom had telephoned and, horrible as his thoughts were – for Bob was over there lying on the sofa, staring mildly at him with kindly eyes – after her call, thoughts number four and five began to make sense.

A private chopper, a private and discreet pilot! With those, the idea of packing and ejecting the dog could work.

Of course he could not even think of physically killing the animal with his own hands or instruments; but drug him, sedate him, pack him in some container and throw the lot out of the chopper… Why not?

But why, oh why, oh why. Why *me*? Max walked up and down the living room of his OzTech-owned apartment. The dog followed his footsteps; his footsteps followed the path dictated by the presence of three MetrePaks delivered that morning – Inge must have arranged it – that would transport all his possessions to OzBase.

All his possessions! They would fill only one and a half, at most, of the MetrePaks. Books, discs, a few clothes, toilet things, a microwave oven… What a small life I have led, thought Max.

The MetrePaks! That was the answer. So obvious. Two MetrePaks for himself, one for the dog.

He pulled the lid off a Pak and inspected its interior. No problem. Buy a ring shackle to clip round that upright *there*; and a clip, a length of chain. The dog, though sedated, would have to be restrained when it awoke. If the lid of a MetrePak could be removed at all, a frantic animal would certainly find a way. And the dog *would* be frantic when the drug wore off. Frantic! Frantically pawing at the slippery metal walls of the MetrePak...! Max shuddered.

He went shopping for the things needed to restrain Bob. It would not after all, Max reflected, be so terrible a death. The drug would put the dog in a coma. The bitter Arctic cold would renew that coma. The dog would suffer only briefly, perhaps not at all, as the last, icy sleep overtook it.

For some minutes Max felt better, or no worse. But fresh panics kept assailing him. Do all OzTech choppers have winches? Yes, of course they do – they all drop and pick up loads, mostly packed MetrePaks. Definitely all choppers have winches: no problem dropping Bob's MetrePak.

But suppose the pilot asked awkward questions? No, most unlikely. It was to be *her* personal pilot and nobody dared question *her* orders.

But suppose...

But, but, but. There was no escape.

The chopper was small, noisy and vibrated so much that Max's brain shook in his head. But it was shaken even before the flight began. What was he doing? What was "right"? Did the word "right" have any meaning?

Surely it could not be "right" to destroy a fine and complex creature, one of God's creations? (But that would not do: what did he mean by "God"?)

Surely it could not be "right" to do away with the dog? But wait: was it a minor freak, or a major phenomenon? Was it just an overnight sensation or a permanent threat to the human race?

What was "right"?

The chopper blattered on and on. Under it, green landscapes turned to grey-and-white deserts. The pilot spoke for the first time. "Getting colder," he said, and switched heaters on.

Now the landscape glared whiter than ever. Ice, snow, bergs. Snow, more snow.

They must be nearing OzBase. Still Max's mind whirled like the blades of the chopper.

Something stirred inside the MetrePak. The dog! It had been drugged. Was it waking up?

And there it was! – OzBase! – directly below!

Now Max had to decide.

He tapped the pilot's shoulder and said one word, "Winch." He was afraid to say more. The awakening dog might recognize his voice.

"OK, winch."

A hatch in the mid-section of the chopper

grated open. Air, unbelievably cold, rushed in. The pilot flipped switches, heater fans blasted, but the outside air won. Tiny frozen particles whirled and settled on the pilot, on Max, on the MetrePak that was to be a tomb.

"Where?" the pilot said, jerking his thumb at the MetrePak.

The dog whined. Max, horrified by the sound, could not answer.

"We don't unload it at the Base, right? She said you wouldn't want that, right? So where?"

"Go round again," Max managed to say. Again the dog whined.

"Oh, come on! It's *cold*. Or haven't you noticed?"

"All right, there. Down there, drop it there."

"You're sure that's what you want?"

"There."

The winch drum screamed, the MetrePak swung away outwards. The winch screamed a different note and the steel cable glistened as it slid through shackles and sheaves. The MetrePak descended.

The pilot said, "OK to drop?" and put a hand on the release lever. "Yes ... no ... hang on," Max said.

"Do I release or don't I?" the pilot shouted furiously.

Max watched, through half-frozen eyes that hurt, the cube of the MetrePak, looking very small now, spinning one way then another, far below.

"Do it!" Max said. "Do it now!"

"What? What?" yelled the pilot. "OK to release?"

"OK, OK," Max called back. But it wasn't OK, nothing was OK, it was all a nightmare.

The pilot pulled the lever. The cable, relieved of its load, writhed like a silver snake. The MetrePak thumped down and sent up a small explosion of powder snow that almost at once blew away sideways.

The cable drum whirred and whined. The steel cable coiled across the drum as it reeled in. Finally the hatch slid shut and, very rapidly, the cabin warmed.

And that was it. Or so Max thought.

Then Madi and Jonjo discovered good dog Bob, the dog that talked.

BOB'S BUBBLES

Jonjo returned to OzBase alone. His mother left him to go to San Francisco for yet another conference.

"What was it like in England?" Madi said. "Tell me all about everything!"

"Oh, great. Terrific. Whammo," Jonjo said.

"Whammo? That's a new one."

"Rhymes with 'ammo'. That was the best bit, using real guns and real ammo!"

"Who used them? *You?* I don't believe you. They don't let little boys use guns!"

"Cut the little-boy stuff. They gave me a gun and I used it and it was great!"

"Did you shoot anyone in particular? Or just blaze away at random?"

"It wasn't *people*, stupid. Rats! Billions of them! Rats everywhere! And there I was with this two-two repeating rifle, a little beauty, a Mannlicher Marksman —"

"I don't believe any of this. *Where* were you?"

"In my hotel bedroom! Honestly! My window looked out on the hotel services area. Mum had a glamorous room with a view. But I'd got a view too, oh yes! All those garbage containers, you know."

"Those big plasticky things? But they're sealed, rats can't get into them."

"Can't they just? These super-rats, you've no idea... Wow, they're clever! You should have seen them, they climb up each others' backs and yatter to each other and work out how to undo the handles —"

"They yatter to each other? You mean, talk?"

"They never stop! Eeek-eek-squeak, yatter yatter chatter! You'd never believe – first they'd clamber over each other to reach the handles, then they'd form a great hanging chain, a cluster like a bunch of grapes, hundreds of them, hanging from the handle. And eventually you'd see the handle move! And that's when your big brudderkins went into action! Blam-blam-blam with the old Mannlicher Marksman! I'd aim for the rats right at the very top of the chain – you should have heard them squeak! – and then the whole chain would collapse, and —"

"You're revolting. You're sick."

"No, I'm not. I'm sane and healthy. And so are a lot of other people, thanks to me. Don't you see, once the rats got to the garbage, the whole city was at risk! Bubonic plague, rabies, you name it."

"I still think it's disgusting, horrid."

"It was great. I spent hours and hours at it. So did the others."

"What others?"

"You don't think I was alone, do you? Haven't you seen any TV or read any papers? Haven't you heard of 'super-rats', 'chatterats'?"

"Of course I know about them but I didn't believe —"

"You'd have believed a hundred per cent if you'd been with Mum and me in that hotel! A five-star hotel, too! Rats, rats everywhere, and special extra staff doing what I was doing, firing out of windows and through doorways with mesh guards to keep the rats out. But they got in all right, there was always some woman yelling, 'Eeek! There's a great *rat* in my bathroom!' and the ROs would rush in and bang-bang, then there'd be thumps and squeals."

"ROs, what are ROs?"

"Rodent Operatives. They've got regiments of them – uniforms and everything. Special ratproof leather gloves and boots, face masks, goggles, the lot. Of course, I was safe in my room, I didn't need all the gear, just the gun. I'm a crack shot."

"You're horrible."

"I'm noble and good and heroic. Blam blam blam! Tell me about Bob."

She began telling him. Once he was satisfied that Bob was safe and well, he hardly listened. "Talking of dogs," he interrupted, "you'd never believe what they're doing! All over Europe, not just where we were. Dogs ganging up! Forming packs! I saw two packs, once from a train and once when we were zooming along a motorway. You'd never believe —"

"You keep saying I'd never believe. And I don't. You're exaggerating, aren't you?"

"Am I? Or is it that the authorities are scared stiff and don't want to let too many stories go public, and start everyone panicking?"

"I don't believe that ordinary dogs would leave their nice comfortable homes and run wild in packs."

"Yes, but there must be lots of extraordinary dogs about. I suppose they haven't had nice comfortable homes. All I know is, there *are* packs of warrior dogs – I've seen them. And I'll tell you something else: they talk to each other. They really do, you can see them doing it. They hold conferences and things."

"Speaking perfect Norwegian, or French, or English, I suppose?"

"No, idiot. They speak in Dogtalk. They put their heads close together and make doggy noises, Mum's doing lots of research on it. And there's always a top dog. The others shut up and he tells them what to do."

"What do they do?"

"They take over. They find some small

village, some place with just a few people in it and they take it over."

"You mean, they kill people?"

"They don't seem to be interested in the people. Not *yet*. They go for farm animals and livestock. They crash into kitchens and open fridges – they can do that! – and eat anything that's going. Then they move on and do it all over again somewhere else."

"Why isn't it shown on telly?"

"I told you, it's hushed up. Why cause a panic?"

"But *you*'ve heard about it, of course! I suppose you're someone special!"

"I'm not. Mum is. Get it?"

Madi was silenced. Now she knew Jonjo was telling her the truth, Mum *would* know the stories: it was her job to hear, investigate and suggest action. And Mum would not bother to hide the facts from her son. She would answer any questions he asked her coldly, clearly and matter-of-factly.

Madi stayed silent, thinking. Then she said, "Jonjo, all this stuff about animals that talk, animals that take over ... it really is true, isn't it?"

"It really is."

"And Bob. Bob talks, doesn't he?"

"Yes, of course he does, he's a sort of pioneer. Dr Lindstrom's prize creation."

"It's frightening, isn't it?" Madi said.

"Yes."

"Jonjo ... is *Bob* frightening?"

Jonjo took time to answer. "Not to *us*," he said finally.

Bob had taken a snooze. Now he awoke, scratched, shook his ears and served himself a snack by pressing a button in the Snomobile's galley. A nozzle made a slurping noise and discharged dog food into a plastic bowl.

Bob ate the food and said, "Bob good dog." He was pleased with himself because he had nudged the bowl into exactly the right position beneath the nozzle. In the past, food had often slopped on to the floor instead of into the bowl. Bob had not minded this but Madi had. She had called him "Bad Dog", "Dirty Dog". Bob understood Madi's words: so, nowadays, he made no mistakes. The food was dropped into the exact middle of the bowl. Good dog.

Having eaten, Bob wondered what to do next. Madi would come later, probably with bones. He liked bones but he loved Madi. He loved her and she loved him. She said so in words. Nowadays, he could reply in words. He was glad and proud about this.

Meanwhile, there were hours to fill. He decided to go to the narrow tunnel that contained his playthings.

He padded through the great cave; paused at the Wishing Well to sniff its strange smell, unlike any earth-smell he had ever encountered; then entered the ever narrowing tunnel that led to his playthings.

He had to scrabble on his belly for the last metre or so, the way in was so small.

Once through this bottleneck, he could stand erect, shake his ruff and wag his tail. For now he was in a glittering, palely-lit ice chamber, bigger than the interior of the Snomobile. The floor was made of ice that became slippery in the centre into which the whole floor dipped, in the same way as the floor of a shower cabinet dips to its lowest point, the plug hole.

In a shower, the dip lets bubbly water out. But in Bob's place, the hole – about grapefruit-size – let bubbly water in. The water came from somewhere deep inside the earth. It was warm and fizzy. Every now and then, it released bubbles, big bubbles, whole families of bubbles. But you had to wait. Bob waited.

Ah, here they were! Clusters of them! Bob jumped to his feet and sprang at them. "Good!" he grunted – and leaped from his hind legs high in the air. *Snap!* – and a big bubble popped! *Snap!* – three bubbles at one go!

Soon, the hole stopped releasing bubbles. Bob knew this would happen – it always did. Now the hole lazily filled with fizzy water. Bob watched the water rise and fall and listened to the glugging noises. He licked his chops, enjoying the strange, unearthly taste left by the bubbles he had caught.

He looked up at the roof of his chamber. There was a hole in it, an ice-lined chimney. Through it he saw grey sky and some of the bubbles he had not caught. Filled with warm gases, the bubbles rose into the sky, lazily spinning and turning, veering when the wind caught them. Up and up they went, some of them bursting, the rest dwindling to almost nothing as they rose still higher. At last, they were so far away that they merged into the greyness and disappeared.

Bob did not mind. He rested his muzzle on his front legs and waited for the next crop of bubbles.

He knew that they would come. They were, like Madi, reliable visitors.

"I can't believe there's anything to be frightened about in Bob," Madi said to Jonjo.

"I don't know what's frightening and what isn't any more," Jonjo said. "I've seen so many weird things."

"Go on, tell," Madi said.

"Well, when Mum and I flew over the extreme northern bits, there was grey-green stuff where it should have been all white and icy."

"That's not weird," Madi said. "That was

just tundra growing. Because of the ice-caps warming up and the climate changing."

"Bet you don't know what 'tundra' means."

"Mini-forests. Tiny vegetation on frozen ground. Of course I know. Tell me something exciting, tundra's boring."

"It's not boring, it's vit-ally im-port-ant," Jonjo said.

"You're trying to sound like Dad."

"No, seriously... Everything's changing so fast. Warming up. The seas getting warmer, swelling up and invading the land."

"Tell me *dramatic* things."

"All right, I'll tell you about the eastern bit of England. The sunken villages, they were dramatic. Wow!"

"Great, tell me."

"They're producing wine all over the southern half. It's got so warm that they've given up growing cereals and taken up wine grapes, bananas and mangoes and all that tropical stuff. Under plastic, of course, but all the same —"

"The *villages*."

"Oh, all right. You go to the east coast and hire glass-bottomed boats – there's fleets of them for the tourist trade. Great. And we had a boat to ourselves, Mum and I, a lectrilaunch called *Pandora*."

"Never mind the boat. Could you really see houses under the water?"

"You really could. Streets, roads, fences, the lot. It was weird. I mean, whole lumps of East Anglia are just swamped. They couldn't keep the sea out, the tides got higher and higher and the sea invaded, and all the people had to move inland."

"You could see houses and churches?"

"Everything was just as it was left. You could look down the chimneys of houses, even. See everything: old bikes that had been left behind, the old-style petrol cars they used before Dieselecs came in, even a motor coach. All rusting to nothing. In one place you could still read the signs on the shops."

"I wish I'd been there! It must have been marv!"

Jonjo did not reply at once. Then he said, "It wasn't really. It was sort of sad. But I couldn't stop looking."

"I'd have loved it!"

"I don't think so. After a time, you felt as if ... as if you were spying ... seeing things you're not supposed to see. A kid's trike ... a garden with bean poles up – well, almost up. Some were still standing, the string was still on them. You know, for runner beans. And a chicken run with wire mesh. And then the sea came in, and the people had to pack up and leave everything behind."

"I hadn't thought of it like that."

Jonjo said, "There were so many things

under the water ... people's lawn-mowers, and a pub with benches still outside it, and stacks of empties at the back. And the inn sign still hanging. I don't know, I felt sort of sick."

Madi kept quiet. Jonjo said, "You could see everything so clearly. The beaches... They were still proper beaches, with railings and promenades and stuff. But all under water, shallow water you could see straight through. You looked at it and half expected to see holiday people walking about. But there weren't any people any more."

Madi looked at her brother and said, "Talk about something else."

Jonjo said, "OK. Let's go and see Bob."

GOLD AND GLORY

They had to pass the lounge to get to the Snowster park. They stopped at the lounge because something unusual was going on. Someone was making a speech and everyone else was standing around with glasses ready to drink a toast.

Madi and Jonjo went in. The Executive Director of OzBase was doing the talking.

"The Nomination is, in itself, an honour and a tribute," he said. "And if the Nomination is confirmed – and we may feel confident that it will be! – each one of us here at OzBase will be able to boast, in years to come, 'Oh yes, I used to work with that distinguished person! Yes, I worked with *the winner of a Nobel Prize!*'"

Laughter and applause. Madi whispered to Jonjo, "Nobel Prize? What's that?"

"Greatest honour you can get, stupid. Nobel Prizes for Science, Arts, work for peace and all that. Big deal, biggest there is. Shut up and listen."

"*Who's* getting a Nobel Prize?"

"Shut up and listen."

"...So let us all raise our glasses," the Executive Director continued, "and drink a

99

toast to one who is shortly to receive world acclaim for her contribution to science –"

"*Her* contribution!" Madi hissed. "He can't be talking about —"

"Shut *up*!" Jonjo growled.

A forest of glasses was raised and clinked. From the centre of the forest rose a solitary figure, lifted above the crowd to stand on a chair.

Dr Inge Lindstrom.

She smiled luminously, waved her hands modestly and spoke.

"In English is a saying, very wise, about chickens!" she began. "The chickens are not to be counted, yes? – before they are hatching!"

Laughter.

"My chicken is not yet hatching. I am only *nominated* for the Nobel, please remember! But let us not waste good champagne. Drink by all means, but let us drink to each other!"

She tilted her golden glass, arched her golden throat and drank. So did everyone else – except one small, undistinguished, uneasy man.

Max, of course.

Madi and Jonjo got him away from the crowd. He went willingly.

"What's it all mean, Max?" Madi said.

"You heard. An international jury of scientists has nominated her for a Nobel Prize."

"Does that mean she actually *gets* it?"

"They don't tell you you're nominated if they don't mean you to get it."

"What's she getting the prize *for*?" Jonjo said. "Is it for being a founder-director of OzTech?"

"No, not for that," Max said. He swigged the remains of his champagne as if it were poison.

"Then what *is* it for?"

"Take a deep breath," Max said. "She's getting it for her pioneer work towards the furtherance of understanding and communication between humans and animals."

"But – but – that's crazy, it's all upside down!" Jonjo stuttered. "She *tortures* animals!"

"She's getting a prize for creating *monsters*?" Madi said.

Max said, "Precisely. She produces a threat – something so evil that it frightens even her. Then she gets a Nobel Prize for it."

"But it's mad, insane!" Madi said. "Couldn't *you* do something?"

"I could drink a large whisky," Max said. "On an occasion like this, champagne sticks in my gullet."

They went to see Bob. He greeted Jonjo by charging at him with such enthusiasm that

Jonjo fell over. Bob licked his face. "Stop it, you great loony!" Jonjo said. "If you want to say hello, say it in words!"

"Ha-yo!" Bob said. "Ha-yo Jawjo!"

"But that's terrifico!" Jonjo said. "Say some more!"

"Bob good dog," Bob said.

"No, say new things!" Madi told Bob. "All your new words!"

"Bones," Bob said. "Fooo-ood. WAW-tuh. Walk. Madi." The words were choked out, bitten, coughed, growled; but you could understand them all right.

"He's the one that should get the Nobel Prize!" Madi said, cuddling Bob.

"Oh, I don't know!" Jonjo said. "I mean, who *created* Bob?"

He was teasing Madi. She took it seriously. She glared at Jonjo, cuddled Bob still more tightly and said, "That pig of a woman...! That Inge Lindstrom!"

Bob heard Inge's name and cowered in Madi's arms.

Bob tried to lead Madi and Jonjo to his bubbles, but the narrow tunnel was much too small. Bob showed his disappointment. His tail drooped. He said "But ... but ... want you *see*!" He was shivering with earnestness and cold. Madi and Jonjo often wondered how he stood the chill of the cave. "Fur," Jonjo said.

"Poor old baldies like us humans wouldn't last a minute."

"Can't you tell us what's in there, Bob?" Madi said. Bob tried but could not make sense. Madi had an idea. "I know what, Bob!" she said. "Jonjo and I will go up on top of the cave, right? And you keep giving little barks so that we know where you are, OK?"

Bob tried to work this out. Jonjo said, "We'll be up *there*," (he jabbed a finger upwards) "and you'll be down *here*, going woof-woof."

Bob said, "Good! Good!" and wagged his tail.

"And then perhaps we'll see things, good things, Bob things," Madi said.

Madi and Jonjo went back through the cave, through the Snomobile and up the ladder. They left Bob behind. Once above ground, they started walking in what they hoped was the right direction.

"I'm cold, so cold, my face is falling off!" Madi said. The wind cut at them. Fortunately it was not strong. "We're morons, doing this!" Madi grumbled. "We don't know what we're looking for!"

But then they heard Bob's barking, their homing-in signal.

They saw before them a tumbledown collection of white rocks – but of course they were not rocks, they were jagged chunks of ice that some inner earth-force had long ago pushed up.

"There he goes again!" Madi said. "Bob! Barking away, regular as clockwork!" They climbed the ice "rocks". They soon reached the top.

Then they saw the big hole in the middle, the mouth of the icy chimney. It flared like the bell of a trumpet. "Ouch!" Jonjo said to Madi. "Go easy! Slip down inside that, and we'd be jammed in the narrow part for ever and ever!"

"Bob would get us out," Madi said.

"He wouldn't," Jonjo said. "He couldn't. We'd be ice fossils stuck down the plughole!"

Madi shouted, "Bob! Bob! We're here! Can you hear me? Bark three times, Bob! One, two, three!"

From the chimney came three hollow "woofs". Then, at intervals, more woofs. But nothing more.

"Terrific," Jonjo said. "We're in contact, we're here and he's there. Now will someone tell me what we're here for?"

Madi said, "Well, there must be *something*, Bob wouldn't let us down."

"Oh, wouldn't he? My nose is freezing, let's go back."

At that moment, Bob began barking shrilly, rapidly, excitedly.

And from the mouth of the chimney, the first bubbles arose.

The bubbles rushed upwards, wobbling fatly, bumping into each other as if racing each other to escape. When they freed themselves from the draught of the chimney, they rose more sedately, as if they had become middle-aged and respectable.

Jonjo muttered, "I don't believe it! Bubbles! *What* bubbles, *why* bubbles?"

Below them, they heard Bob bark and scrabble delightedly.

"Why don't they burst?" Madi said. "Bubbles always burst." Like Jonjo, she could hardly believe what she was seeing.

"They're not ordinary bubbles, just look at them! They've got something stuck inside them at the bottom."

If you looked carefully, you could see what he meant. Each bubble carried a tiny cargo, a dark thing or cluster of things no bigger than grape pips.

The wind gusted and veered. Bubbles flurried sideways and flung themselves at Madi's face. Some of them burst. "Yeuck!" she cried, wiping her face with her gloved hands. "Filthy pong! Filthy gassy smell! And they're slimy! Yeuck!"

"Calm down, calm down, let me." He wiped her face clean of the bubbles' wetness.

The moisture felt oily, soapy. The smell the burst bubbles had left behind was like nothing he had ever known: earthy, gassy, sulphurous, all kinds of things.

"Horrible!" Madi said.

"Yes, maybe, but hang on," said Jonjo. "Let's do some bubble-hunting." He moved into the main line of the bubbles' flight and let them burst against him. "Haven't we got anything to trap them in?" he said.

"Yeuck, the stuff's all over me –"

"We've got to collect samples of the gas and the pip things."

"How can we? We haven't got – no, wait, I've got this plastic bag, I used it for Bob's bones. But it won't be any good, it's full of bone pong."

"Use it anyhow. Catch a bubble in it. Go on!"

"*There*…! And another, *there*!"

"Keep going."

"You do it, I hate the smell."

He trapped a dozen or more bubbles. As they burst, they formed dribbles of faintly brown liquid in the plastic bag. Their cargo, the pip-like things, gathered wetly in the bottom of the bag. He twisted the bag's neck and sealed it with a knot. "That should do," he said.

"Do for what?"

"Do for analysis," Jonjo said. "We've got to

know what the bubbles are, what they're for, why they exist."

"They don't have to have a reason," Madi said.

"But suppose they have! Suppose they're a vital clue to something or other! – the ultimate breakthrough in what's-its-name, ta-ra!"

"If they are, just remember that it was Bob who discovered them. Darling, clever Bob!"

"Cut the gush," said Jonjo. Then, "Look, they're stopping. No more bubbles. Let's go back to Bob and give him a bone."

FLIGHT OF FANCY

In OzBase, crazes broke out from time to time. Three-dimensional chess, electronic pool and snooker, building snowmen, gambling – anything to break the monotony of life.

As soon as Madi and Jonjo had parked their Snowster, they were made aware of the latest craze. In the lounge, Karl – leader of the Snomobile rescue – pounced on them.

"Binoculars!" he shouted. "Got to have binocs! Jonjo, Madi, do you have —"

"What would I want with binoculars?" Madi said.

"Never mind that, have you *got* them?"

"No. Jonjo had a telescope once — "

"Jonjo, my dear old pal! Lend me your telescope!" Karl said.

"I chucked it away yonks ago. It was just a toy, all blurry. Anyhow, what's all this about? Why binoculars?"

"Haven't you heard? Tomorrow, the aerial circus comes to town! The Big Show!"

"*What* big show?" Madi said.

"Balloons! Dr Stepan's balloons! Hundreds of them! Thousands!"

"You mean Dr Stepan who helped rescue

us?" Madi said. "Why is he playing with balloons?"

"He's got squadrons of balloons carrying ozone bullets!" Karl explained. "Ozone, to patch up the hole in the Ozone Layer."

"Sounds mad," Jonjo said. "Just a flight of fancy, ha-ha."

Madi said, "Seriously, will it do any good?"

"Ask Stepan – he's over there," Karl said. "All I care about is that there'll be something to *see*, something *happening*. You're sure you haven't got binocs?"

Madi and Jonjo went over to Dr Stepan. "Everyone is raving about your balloons," Madi said. "Please explain." Carefully, for he was a serious and eminent scientist, he told them about his balloons. They were to carry and discharge factory-produced ozone "bullets". They were the product of an international consortium. This was to be the first of many such balloon flights.

When he had finished, Madi said, "Wow! Do you think it will work?"

Dr Stepan gave her question his full consideration. He fingered his chin, pursed his lips and stared at the ceiling.

"Well, will it?" Jonjo said.

"I shouldn't think so," Dr Stepan replied at last.

Whether they worked or not, the balloons

made a magnificent spectacle. And the inhabitants of OzBase were lucky: the sullen low cloud that so often hid the sky was almost absent. You could look upwards into the heavens.

"Here they come!" people told each other, as the first glints appeared over the horizon. The glints became pear-shaped, coloured objects – a solemn procession of marching balloons, each obeying every shift of wind with the identical bob or curtsey or spin.

"Oooh!" people said. "Aaah!" It was like watching fireworks.

The procession went on and on, heading for a distant, invisible destination high up in the sky where the balloons' ozone bullets would be discharged and the hole in the Ozone Layer would be cured.

Or not cured. Everyone hoped but nobody knew.

The aerial circus, the greatest show on earth, was over all too soon. Nothing followed it. Days filled with nothing in particular came and went. Inge flew to America to star in a mega-dollar TV science series. She left nothing behind her except an emptiness: now there was no beautiful woman to brighten the eyes and smiles of the men and no villain for Max, Madi and Jonjo to hate. Inside OzBase, everything seemed grey and lifeless. Outside, the weather settled into a pattern that would interest only a meteorologist – no seasonal storms, no ferocious, icy gales, no icy clamp-down.

Just nothing in particular.

For Madi and Jonjo, the settled weather was a blessing. It meant that they could continue to use the Snowster and visit Bob. But the general feeling of nothing-in-particular seemed to have reached even him. He was subdued. His tail wagged less vigorously. His attention wandered sooner during his Word Lessons.

"We shouldn't be surprised," Madi said to Jonjo. "I mean, it's not much of a life for him, is it? Just waiting for us to turn up... Then back to eating, sleeping and more waiting."

"We bring him new toys and everything," Jonjo said. "I don't see what more we can do."

Madi said, "He's too clever to be put off with playthings. But at least we tried."

And they had tried. They had brought Bob Surprise Packets: to get to the bone wrapped deep in the packet, Bob had to solve little puzzles and speak certain words. The Surprise Packets were electronic puzzles, crammed with hi-tech ingenuities. It had taken Max, Jonjo and Madi many hours to invent and construct them. Usually it took Bob only minutes to solve them. Or worse, he lost interest. The packet might remain unopened, or simply be torn apart.

"He's still got his bubbles," Jonjo said. "He still likes waiting for them and catching them when they start up."

"I wish we could watch him doing it," Madi said. "It would be great if we could open up the tunnel and crawl in there to be with him."

"If we had ham, we could have ham and eggs," Jonjo said grumpily. "If we had some eggs…"

Madi gave a scornful "ha-ha" and fiddled with her multi-layered suit. Jonjo looked gloomy and did nothing. Then he said, "Let's give Bob the latest news on the bubbles! That might interest him!"

Madi lay on the floor of the Snomobile with an arm round Bob's neck. "Those bubbles of yours, Bob, you'd never believe what we've done! Are you listening, Bob?"

He wagged his tail half-heartedly.

"Remember that day when we went up there, outside, and you chased the bubbles up to us? Remember that, Bob?"

Bob said, "Yush."

"Yush" was better than his old "Yes" sound, "Ye-ap", but it was still not perfect.

"Say *Yes*, Bob. Go on, I know you can. *Yes, yes*."

"Yush."

"Oh well, never mind. Do you want to hear about the bubbles, Bob?"

"Bob good dog."

"Of course you are. Well, we collected some bubbles in a plastic bag. They burst, of course, but we got what was left – the gas inside them and the wet stuff they were made of, and the little pip things they carried —"

"You don't expect him to understand all that, do you?" Jonjo said crossly.

"Of course he understands, don't you, Bob?" Madi said.

"Bob good dog," Bob said, and yawned.

"I'm glad you're so interested," Madi said. "Well, the next thing we did was to hand over all the stuff to Max."

"Max, yush," Bob said. He freed himself from Madi's arm and gave himself a good shaking.

"Listen, Bob. Pay attention. We gave all the bubble stuff to Max, and he's finding out what the bubbles are *for*, what they're *made* of, everything! Isn't that terrific!"

Bob stopped shaking himself. At last he seemed interested. He stared at her and said, "Bub-bools, yush! What for, bub-bools?"

Jonjo and Madi exchanged glances. "Well, actually," Jonjo said at last, "Max hasn't come up with anything yet. But he was very interested, really he was."

"Thrilled to bits," Madi said sarcastically. "Over the moon. Chuffed as anything, oh yes..."

"What Max say?" Bob insisted.

113

"Well, nothing, *yet*," Madi admitted.

"But any moment now…" Jonjo said, trying to sound bright and lively.

Bob looked from Madi to Jonjo and back again; then gave a snort and turned his back on them.

And so the visit to Bob wore on. Nothing in particular happened.

In OzBase's lounge, they looked for Max and failed to find him. "Max – where's he gone?" Madi asked Dr Stepan.

"I don't know. He left on the Tuesday chopper. What's today?"

"Wednesday," Jonjo said.

"Yes, of course. All the days seem the same here… Yes, he went yesterday."

"Where to? Oslo?"

"Oslo, London. Paris… What's the difference?"

"Did he say anything? Was he carrying anything with him?"

"I do not notice such things. You would like a drink? Coke? Orange?"

"No. But thank you."

Jonjo said, "I don't understand Max. I mean, it's so *rude*! – just taking our bubble stuff, and promising to get it analysed and everything, and then not telling us anything! Really gross!"

"Well, he's like that," Madi said. "A bit of a squit. He never showed much interest in the bubbles."

"He did when we first told him about them. And when we handed over our specimens."

"I suppose he did. He grilled us for half an hour, didn't he? All sorts of questions. Then – nothing. Not a word."

"I suppose he's got other things on his mighty mind," Jonjo said. "Great psychological problems to solve, like exactly how he feels when his laundry comes back with one sock missing."

"I think shrinks stink," Madi said. "Try saying that three times quickly! Bet you can't!"

Jonjo tried and failed. The tongue-twister was amusing for all of two minutes. But no longer.

And then Max was back, and nothing-in-particular became everything-extraordinary.

Max did not even look like Max. His face was alive. His voice was urgent.

"This is Madi, and this is Jonjo, and this is Dr Reeves Manningham," he said, making everyone shake hands with everyone else. "*The* Dr Reeves Manningham," Max went on. "You must have heard of him – "

Dr Reeves Manningham was so big, tanned, relaxed and handsome in a plug-ugly way that he made Madi nervous. "You're the one who knows about climates and things," Madi said, deliberately making herself sound silly. "Mum has talked about you, I think."

"Climates and things," Reeves said. "Yes, that's about it." He looked at Madi with penetrating green eyes and smiled. She looked away.

"Ask the doctor what brought him to OzBase!" Max said.

"All right," said Madi. "What brought you to OzBase, Dr Reeves Manningham?"

"You did," he replied. "You two, your dog Bob – and Bob's bubbles."

"Bob's supposed to be a secret!" Madi flared. "Max! – we agreed not to tell anyone about him!"

"Dr Reeves isn't anyone," Max said. "He's your best friend, Madi. Yours too, Jonjo. And most of all, Bob's."

Madi said, "Everyone's best friend. Isn't that nice. And nobody's enemy, I suppose?"

"Only one enemy!" Max said and laughed. Madi and Jonjo did not know why. Till later.

"Put it in plain language," Jonjo said to Dr Reeves, twenty minutes later. "I haven't understood a word. Nor has Madi."

"Oh, yes I have, I've understood everything!" Madi said, looking at Dr Reeves. Jonjo could tell that she wanted to impress him. Maliciously, he said, "Well, Madi, *you* explain it all to me! Go on!"

"Yes, well, it's all quite simple really," she said. "There's a hole in the Ozone Layer, right? And it's got to be mended, or the whole world will be in trouble, right?"

"Brilliant!" Jonjo said. "Fabulous! Tell me more!"

"Oh, shut *up*. Well, there're two things we can do. First we can stop sending up things that attack the ozone – cut down on our use of all the bad gases and vapours and stuff like that ... CFCs, and carbon monoxide and everything –"

"You make it all so clear and simple!" Jonjo said.

"Oh, shut *up*. Well, that's one side of it. Second, we can try to *patch* the hole: replace the ozone. And that's what Dr Stepan's balloons were for, they carried ozone bullets into the layer, and let them off, and —"

"And it didn't work," Jonjo said. "We couldn't get enough ozone up there, or be sure that it hit the right places."

"I'm telling this," Madi said, "aren't I, Dr Reeves?"

"You are, and you're doing fine," he said. "Carry on."

"The only real, proper way to stop the hole spreading," Madi continued, "would be to find a *natural* cure; a cure from the planet itself. You know, like the way sun and rain make plants grow in soil. All *natural*, nothing to do with laboratories or chemicals factories. But it would have to be really big-scale, not like Dr Stepan's balloons, something *enormous*, terrific amounts of ozone –"

"And there'd have to be a foolproof way of getting the ozone up into the Ozone Layer," Dr Reeves said. "That's what you were going to say, wasn't it, Madi?"

"Pre-cisely," Madi said. "But no one's found the answers. So we're in dead trouble. The Hole in the Head keeps getting bigger, and that's tied up with the whole planet and its seas hotting up, the Greenhouse Effect – and *that*'s tied up with changes in plants and animals –"

"Which leads to good dog Bob," said Dr Reeves. "And his bubbles. Bob's bubbles. Oh yes, indeed…"

"I don't see what's so exciting about Bob's bubbles," Jonjo said. "I mean, they're just *bubbles*, and there aren't all that many of them anyhow –"

"Packet of seeds," Max said.

"Packet of seeds?" Jonjo said. "What's that got to do with anything?"

"Buy a packet of seeds – it weighs nothing, costs hardly anything. But with those seeds, you might cover a hectare of ground with living plants."

"And those plants would produce more seeds that would produce more plants next year and the year after," Dr Reeves said. "An endless expanse of green. All from a packet of seeds."

"All right, all right," Jonjo said. He was getting cross. "But the hole in the Ozone Layer is about the size of the USA, right? And something's got to be done *now*, there's hardly any time left –"

"But we've got a packet of seeds," Dr Reeves said.

"I still don't see —"

Max said, "Just listen. Dr Reeves analysed the grape-pip things you found in Bob's bubbles, remember? They are the *seeds*. They are little factories, waiting to start up. When they start up, they produce something more precious than diamonds or rubies or gold. *Ozone*."

"And the bubbles, and the gas in them," Dr Reeves said, "they're the carriers of the seeds, their food, their compost, their womb."

"You came from a womb, Jonjo," Madi said sweetly. "Or was it a tin can? Sometimes you're so dim..."

It was Jonjo's turn to say, "Oh, shut *up*." Then he said, "Seriously, just a few bubbles with a few seeds in them... It can't be the answer! You'd need millions of bubbles, thousands of packets of seeds!"

"Ah," said Dr Reeves, "that's why I'm here. The ecological scientist. Also Chief Bubble Hunter. And in about an hour from now, my team should be arriving. The Bubble Brigade. Oil drills, geophysicists, roustabouts, the lot!"

"Roustabouts?" Madi said.

"Men who work the oil rigs in the oilfields. Men who drill deep holes."

"What will they find at the bottom of the holes?" Jonjo asked.

"Bubbles."

"But how do you know? Why should they find anything at all?"

"True," Dr Reeves said. "But then, those ice-rocks you clambered over to get to the top of Bob's bubble-chimney... how much do you think they weighed?"

"Tonnes and tonnes, I suppose."

"Agreed. Now, what force pushed up those tonnes and tonnes? Just a handful of bubbles?"

"But that could have happened millions of years ago. Probably Bob's bubbles are all that's left over."

Madi said, "Dr Reeves wouldn't come all the way here, with teams of people and everything, if he wasn't quite sure of striking oil. I mean, ozone. You wouldn't, would you, Dr Reeves?"

For once Dr Reeves' face seemed less large and confident.

"Well, you know," he said, "things *can* go wrong. There's always an element of risk..."

ROUSTABOUTS

The choppers blattered and bellowed in the grey-white sky. They came lower and lower – blew great rings of snow as they settled – then lurched to a halt, rotors whining and drooping as the motors were cut.

Men, women and equipment were unloaded. Some of the men were big and tough. You could guess at the muscled arms beneath their layered clothing. Others were careful and earnest. They clutched precious scientific instruments to their chests and hurried to the safety of OzBase reception area.

There were fewer women, but they too formed a mixed bunch. The most striking was Dr Tuula Salmi, six feet tall, ruddy-cheeked, crop-haired. She boomed and guffawed and shouted greetings in Finnish, flailing her arms across her enormous bosom to keep warm. She scorned heated suits. She wore brilliantly coloured ski sweaters and a big woolly hat with a pompom.

"Seismologist," Max told Jonjo and Madi. "Measures earthquakes, tremors, things happening underground. She's the best."

"Does she back up Dr Reeves' ideas about the bubbles?" Jonjo said.

But someone had thrown a snowball at Dr Salmi, and she was furiously counter-attacking, bellowing with laughter, and everyone else was laughing. Even Max.

Snomobiles churned snow and made deep tracks like roads; choppers thrashed and whined, dropping clanking metal from the icy grey sky; yellow-helmetted roustabouts bellowed, "Easy ... keep her coming ... more, more ... OK, cut!"; scientists, engineers and foremen fretted over clipboards and formed into hand-waving, argumentative clusters that kept breaking up and re-forming; generators whined, cable-drums screeched, cranes and derricks shuddered as their metal-plate feet found purchase in the protesting snow and ice –

And up they went – the derricks, the drills, the tools that would pierce the earth's crust and bore deep down into its vitals.

"It's happening so fast!" Madi said. "I mean, just two days ago this place was just a – just a –"

"Pimple in the wilderness," Jonjo suggested.

"And now it's a – it's a —"

"Fairground," Jonjo said. "Roundabouts, roustabouts, I don't know what!"

"Poor Bob," Madi said. "He must be hearing all this racket and wondering what's happening. We'd better go and see him."

"Good thing he speaks English!" Jonjo said. "I'd hate to try and explain all this to an ordinary dog!"

On the third day, the roustabouts suddenly stood still and silent, all looking upwards. Most of them held hot drinks or cold beers in their thickly gloved hands: but none of them drank. They just looked and waited.

Then a starter motor yelped and grated – and another – and the big engines fired and roared and rumbled – and, at the very top of a high lattice tower, a great banana-shaped metal crossbeam jerked.

It jerked, then settled into a clockwork see-saw rhythm, gravely nodding its massive head. Somebody cheered – everybody cheered – and Dr Salmi threw her bobbled woolly hat in the air and did an elephantine jig. Some roustabouts joined in, kicking up powder snow with their big boots.

Others took no notice. They formed a ring round the pump gear at the base of the rig, staring at a sliding steel shaft that also rotated. As it turned, it dug down, driving a toothed and clawed drill-head ever deeper.

An hour went by. And another.

Dr Reeves was there. "When's something going to *happen*?" Madi asked him, almost in a whisper.

"Soon, I hope," he said. "Some time, I trust.

Never, I fear." He grinned, uneasily.

"What's *supposed* to happen?" she asked.

"Fizzing noises. Soda water. A big burp. Who knows?" he said.

Then someone shouted, "Get back!" and people ran from the drill, making a pattern like spokes in a wheel. There was a whistling hiss that became a deafening, gassy screech. The rig shook, the ground trembled – and a white conical cloud burst from the earth into the sky like the steam from the spout of a monster kettle.

Smashed ice rained down in lumps.

Dr Reeves said, "My God!" and pushed Madi behind him.

"I can't see, I want to *see*!" she shouted,

"It's incredible, fantastic, just look at it!" Jonjo yelled.

"But I can't *see*, let me *see*!"

She tore herself free from Dr Reeves. Now she could see the roaring white plume jetting into the grey sky. It looked solid, yet at its topmost height, it faltered, failed, spread outwards into a misty mushroom, then began falling as mist.

The downpour wetted her upturned face. The wetness had a smell to it. She recognized it at once.

The smell of Bob's bubbles.

In the lounge, Dr Salmi said, "Ho ho ho!" and

raised her glass to Dr Reeves. He said, "Ho ho ho!" and clinked his glass against hers.

"Whisky no good," she boomed. "Schnapps better. Ho ho ho!" There were half a dozen little schnapps glasses in front of her and four whisky glasses in front of Dr Reeves. His eyes looked upside down and his smile seemed to wander all over his face. Dr Salmi looked merely cheerful, though bright red. "Ho ho ho!" she said, downing her drink in a single gulp.

"Ho ho ho!" Jonjo said to Madi. He was drinking non-alcoholic beer, which he pretended to like but didn't. She drank her latest craze, passion-fruit juice. "Ho ho ho!" she said.

"It's a good thing Dr Salmi turned up," Jonjo said. "I mean, you can't keep saying 'Congratulations, Dr Reeves, what a triumph!' It's much easier to say 'Ho ho ho!' and keep grinning."

"'Ho ho ho!' says all that needs saying," Madi said.

"Or bubble-ubble-ubble," said Jonjo. He nodded his head at the window. Through the glass, you could see the sky; and in the sky, bubbles. Endless flights of them whirling, swirling, colliding with each other, bossily bumping each other, and always rising, rising, rising, till they reached the Ozone Layer.

"Where's Max?" Madi said.

"I don't know. Out there, I suppose, grinning at the bubbles and making bets on how long it will take them to mend the Hole in the Head. He'll be out at the rig."

But as she spoke, he entered the lounge. For the first time ever, Madi and Jonjo saw him wearing a wide grin. Max smiling! "Surprise, surprise!" Jonjo muttered.

There was a bigger surprise to follow. Max was holding on to something – a leather strap. The seated crowd hid whatever was at the other end of the strap. But then it became visible.

A dog.

Bob.

Madi leapt to her feet, spilling passion-fruit juice. "How could you!" she shouted at Max. "How dare you! I'll kill you for this! Bob's a secret, *our* secret!"

"Not any more," Max said, grinning more widely than ever.

"But you promised, we all agreed," Jonjo began.

"All past history," Max said. "All over now. Down, Bob! Down!"

Too late. Bob had his front legs round Madi's neck and she, half laughing, half furious, spilled the rest of the passion-fruit juice on Jonjo. He hardly noticed. Now Bob was greeting *him*, trying to lick his face.

"What do you mean, 'past history, all over now?'" Madi demanded of Max.

"Obvious, isn't it? Bob *was* a secret, once. Because he had an enemy, a powerful enemy, once. Well, now he's only got friends."

"You mean Inge's dropped dead?" Madi said, hopefully.

"I doubt it. She's indestructible."

"But if she's still around, poor darling Bob is in danger!"

"Oh, come on, Madi! Think! How much longer has Inge got? Assume she's on TV at this moment, right? But will she be a TV star in a week's time? Or will she be selling matches in the street?"

Jonjo said, "Who knows. But she's still the glamour girl of science, isn't she? The Nobel Prize-winner and everything?"

"No," Max said. "She's washed up as a scientist. And she won't get a Nobel Prize."

"Why ever not?"

"Because too many people will come forward to say 'No'. Even me. And because of him: Bob."

Madi had not been listening. She was too busy introducing Bob to his new friends, the scientists in the lounge. "Shake hands properly, Bob!" she said, and Bob offered his paw for another hand to shake. "No, your *right* paw, Bob!"

"Ight paw," Bob said, gravely.

"And this is Smithy, Bob. Say 'Smithy!'"

"Miffy."

"Now say 'Hello, Smithy!'"

"Ah-yo, Miffy." Bob's tail wagged. "Bob good dog?" he asked Madi.

"Of course you are! Best dog in the world!"

Bob took a rest from hand-shaking and began licking up the spilled passion-fruit juice. The more he licked, the faster his tail wagged. "Good!" he said. "Nice – good! More!"

The eminent scientists almost fought for the honour of buying Bob's next round.

SPEECH! SPEECH!

Sweden. The Nobel Prize ceremony.

Everyone was there – the cream of the world's great brains; the men and women chosen by their peers as the cleverest, the worthiest, the greatest.

Bob was there.

Not in the audience, of course; not among the learned gentlemen with sashes across their starched shirt-fronts, or among the eminent ladies who had worried so much about their evening dresses and hair styles. But Bob was there all right, with Madi and Jonjo. Max had smuggled them in. They had an unwanted cloakroom all to themselves. They could hear the orchestra when it played, and the amplified boom of the speechmakers, and the surges of applause. They could not hear them very well, but no matter. They were there.

Applause! Thousands of hands clapping! Then a break, and some muffled words. (In what – German? Italian? French? English?) Then renewed applause as yet another great man or woman walked to the podium to receive an award and make a speech...

"It gets a bit boring, doesn't it?" Jonjo said. "I mean, what are they all on about now?

Human rights, or medicine, or ecology, or what?"

"Drink your champagne," Madi said.

"It's all gone, I only managed to pinch half a bottle. I thought champagne made you drunk, I don't feel drunk. Just thirsty."

"Passion-fruit juice is better," Madi said. "Champagne's all bubbles. How are you, Bob? All right? Oh lor, he's finished all his water. Oh, poor Bob –"

"Don't start that again," Jonjo said. "The way you drivel and slaver over Bob... That crummy band has started up again! This could go on for hours and hours."

They half-listened to the music and beat time on Bob's fur. Bob was not amused. He said, "Home soon?" and Madi said, "Not yet, I'm afraid. There may be something about Max or Dr Reeves, I don't know. A medal or something. I wish I had some passion-fruit juice."

Bob said, "Juice nice, good," and yawned.

And suddenly Max was there, looking all wrong in full formal dress, glistening white shirt-front and slicked-down hair. "Come on, quick! Into the auditorium!"

"They'll chuck us out –"

"No, no, come with me! Just keep low and don't make a sound! Quick!"

They were in the auditorium. A man with a beard was finishing a speech. A good speech:

people were nodding agreement, chuckling, sometimes clapping. "The difficulty is a familiar one," the speechmaker said. "To whom does this award truly belong? Who should receive it? Should it be the person who first 'saw the light' – developed a theory – produced the all-important concept? Or the person who *did* the necessary things – the man or woman of action who turned theory into fact? Or, even – should it be some innocent, unknowing bystander who just happened to be there ... yet was able say, 'Oh, you want every sick person in the world to be well, instantly. Is that all? Well, look in this cardboard box, under my spare pair of socks! There's your answer!'"

Laughter. A rattle of applause.

Madi looked up at Max. He was only half-smiling and worriedly fingering his lower lip.

The speech went on. It was hard to attend to it, there was so much to look at – the wonderful hall, the rows of people all so distinguished, yet all so different in age and appearance, the flute-player who made faces when he blew...

"A cure not merely for sick *people*, but a sick *planet*!" said the speaker.

Jonjo saw the conductor of the orchestra give his tail-coat a quick heave under each armpit. Must be sweaty work, Jonjo thought, waving your arms about under all those lights.

"...the seemingly impossible and insanely

131

complex task of mending a hole in the Ozone Layer," said the speaker.

Madi thought, Headphones: obviously, you'd need them, so many speakers speaking so many languages. That's why everyone's issued with headphones. Wouldn't it be funny if you could jam the system and belt out some rock 'n' roll...!

But now the speaker was naming prizewinners' names. Unbelievable names! Dr Gibbon, and Dr Reeves! And a special citation for Dr Salmi! And Max was sweating and muttering furiously, and trying to hide behind Jonjo and Madi – who were too small to be of any use – and faces, hundreds of them, were swivelling in his, Max's direction, smiling faces – and the applause was growing and growing –

And Max was pulled away from Madi and Jonjo, dragged towards the platform by people with sashes and medals –

And so were Dr Reeves and Dr Salmi, both of them laughing and waving their hands as if to say, "No, not me, you want Max, over there!"

And they were all three of them on the platform having their hands shaken and their cheeks kissed – which Dr Salmi did not mind at all, and Dr Reeves did not mind much, and which Max hated –

And there were microphones on a dais, and

Dr Salmi was thrust in front of them. She beamed and waved at people in the audience and made a speech in Finnish which ended "Ho ho ho!"

And something was thrust into her hands, and a sash was put round her neck, and Dr Reeves replaced her in front of the microphone –

And he made a short, loud, cheerful speech, and was given a scroll, a medal and a sash –

And then it was Max's turn. The main event. The big prize.

He put up a feeble resistance, but there were so many hands pushing at him – so many smiling faces encouraging him – that he lost the fight and stood, shrunken in his formal dress, grey-faced and shiny with sweat, in front of the microphones. His hands dangled. His lips trembled. "Oh, poor Max!" Madi said to Jonjo.

"Poor nothing! He's getting the top gong!"

"Oh, poor Max!" Madi repeated. "He's hating it! They're making him look ridiculous!"

Someone with a beautiful white beard was urging Max to speak. Miserably, Max obeyed.

"Ridiculous!" he mumbled.

"Please!" said the bearded man. "A few words...! Please!"

"Ridiculous!" Max repeated. Now his voice sounded loud and clear. "Surely you can see

133

how ridiculous this is? How can I accept this award? How can any one person?"

"Please!" said the bearded man. "Just a few gracious words of acceptance, nothing more...!"

"I deserve no prizes," Max said. "No single person does. Not even my distinguished colleagues, Dr Reeves Manningham and Dr Tu ... Tuuli ... Dr Salmi..."

"He's forgotten her name!" Madi giggled to Jonjo.

"Ask yourselves," Max continued, "*what* was discovered? Easy answer – the vital means of patching the hole in the Ozone Layer. Next question: *how* was it discovered? Was it by a programme of dedicated scientific research? Certainly not! The great discovery was made by happy accident, nothing more!"

The audience was silent.

"Last, ask yourselves *who* made the great discovery? Which is the same as asking, *who* merits the acclaim of this gathering and the award of its supreme prize? Dr Reeves, Dr Salmi, myself? Of course not! We did not find the magic bubble. We simply chased it.

"So I ask you, who gets the prize? No one answers? Then I must tell you. The true winners are here in this hall, both of them! Yes, there at the back! Don't let them get away! Bring them up here!"

Jonjo said, "Oh no! Let me out!" and started running. Madi swore indistinctly, tried to follow, and fell over Bob. Bob yelped and ran in the wrong direction, ending up under the skirt of a large lady who said, "Mein Gott!" and looked as if she had been stung by a bee.

Meanwhile, Dr Salmi grabbed Jonjo and dragged him – she had a grip like an all-in wrestler's – to the stage; and Dr Reeves picked up Madi and carried her through the audience.

Bob followed, tail down, howling softly.

And there they were, Madi and Jonjo, dazzled by lights and cheering and laughter, fumbling with awards that were thrust into their hands or around their necks.

And Max was bellowing their names into the microphones, shouting out the story of the discovery of the bubbles –

And everyone was happy except Madi, Jonjo and Bob.

Slowly, a roaring storm gathered in the crowd. "Speech!" people shouted, in dozens of languages, "Speech! Speech! Speech!" So Jonjo and Madi had to say something.

They kept interrupting each other. "Max has got it all wrong," Jonjo said. "It was all an accident, we don't deserve any credit —"

"Oh, yes we do!" Madi said. "We found the bubbles, didn't we? If it hadn't been for us —"

"We *didn't* find the bubbles!" Jonjo said. "That's rot, you know it is! —"

"But if we hadn't been there," Madi said, "if we hadn't reported them to Max, so that he got the analysis done, and then Dr Salmi and Dr Reeves did their stuff — "

"Never mind all that, *we* didn't discover the bubbles!" Jonjo said. To the audience, he explained, "Madi's like that. Shoving herself forward. *Typical*. She knows as well as I do who was the *real* discoverer!"

"Oh!" Madi said. "I see what you mean! Yes, of course, dear brother, you're right, as always. My clever brother," she told the audience at large, "is never *wrong*. Ho hum..."

"The proper discoverer," Jonjo shouted, "wasn't Madi and it wasn't me. It was —"

"Oh! – of course! – it was BOB!" Madi said. She tried to hug him but Bob ran under a gilt chair and showed the whites of his eyes.

They managed to drag him out. His legs sprawled all over the place and his paws scrabbled against the microphones, making a terrible noise.

But the noise from the hall was even louder. The audience rose to its feet. "SPEECH, SPEECH!" it thundered, as the Nobel sash with the beautiful medal was put round Bob's furry neck. "Home now?" he whimpered, swivelling appealing eyes from Madi to Jonjo. "Go home?"

"But Bob, you don't understand you're famous, you're top dog in the world!"

"Bob, darling Bob, they all love you, and you've won a medal!"

At last they got Bob to sit on the podium and stop trembling. Though one ear was up and the other down and inside out, he began to understand what was happening. He even wagged his tail very slightly.

"They're waiting!" Jonjo whispered into Bob's drooping ear, turning it right way round. "You've got to make a speech!"

"Say something, anything!" Jonjo begged.

Bob sniffed at the microphones. Amplified sniffing noises filled the hall. Bob liked the effect. He sniffed some more.

"*Say* something!" Jonjo said.

The audience quietened. Some people even sat down. Bob shook his ruff, licked his lips and settled himself more comfortably on the podium, preparing to make the speech that marked one of the great moments in the history of the planet Earth.

Complete silence: then Bob spoke.

"Bob good dog," he said, then jumped down into Madi's lap.

The applause lasted exactly four minutes by Max's watch.

AFTER ALL

Outside and beyond the great hall where the ceremony was held, the world gradually changed.

Over the years the ice-caps re-froze. The trade winds resumed their old, familiar patterns. The rats went underground. Dogs forgot to form packs and returned to their old domestic lives, curling up for a snooze in the best armchairs. The swollen seas receded and people moved back into their coastal homes. Northern Europe's stormy winters and stifling, impossible summers gradually became old history.

Max retired and raised a prize-winning strain of sweet peas, "Gibbon Grandees".

Jonjo became a wind-farmer, and seriously rich.

Madi raised five children, and numerous border collies in the kennels she and her husband ran.

A statue of Bob ("Our World Saviour!" as a cheap newspaper called him) was commissioned and actually completed. Unfortunately the sculptor was not very good at dogs. Bob looked as if he were sitting on a thistle. The statue must be lying around somewhere.

Dr Inge Lindstrom – whatever became of her? Nobody seems to know.

In the Arctic and Antarctic, there were still OzBase and its equivalents, manned by bored scientists. They watched and reported on bubbles (now called Bobbles, in honour of Bob).

They shivered, grumbled and put up with the ageing huts, the horizon-less icy bleakness, the flitter and swirl of powdery snow around their ankles...

And the sight of the Bobbles, always ascending, sometimes tumbling like clowns, as they soared to the Ozone Layer.